tangle
GIRLS

tangle GIRLS

Edited By

Nicole Kimberling

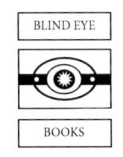

Blind Eye Books
blindeyebooks.com

Tangle Girls
Edited by Nicole Kimberling

Published by:
Blind Eye Books
1141 Grant Street
Bellingham, WA 98225
blindeyebooks.com

All rights reserved. No part of this book may be used or reproduced in any manner without written permission of the publisher, except for the purpose of reviews.

Edited by Nicole Kimberling
Cover art by Sam Dawson

All stories within this anthology are works of fiction and as such all characters and situations are fictitious. Any resemblances to actual people, places or events are coincidental.

First edition January 2009
Copyright 2009
Printed in the United States of America.

ISBN 978-0-9789861-4-8

Library of Congress Control Number: 2008911135

This book is dedicated to amazons and activists everywhere.

Introduction

I love Wonder Woman. I love her hair and her boots and her boomerang tiara. And I love that she lives (or used to live, in the 70's television series) on the Isle of the Amazons. Oh, how my young mind was filled with images of that tropical island of feisty toga-clad women. I wore a toga for Halloween for five years and no one knew why. To be fair, even I didn't know why exactly. My awareness of being a lesbian had not progressed to the point that I was able to understand that I was attracted to Princess Diana. I just knew that I was always disappointed when Steve Trevor entered the picture and perplexed by Diana's devotion to him when she had all those beautiful Amazons waiting for her back home.

Here in Tangle Girls I've collected stories featuring heroines who are not only worthy of fighting alongside my old idol but who are unafraid to return the affection of their fellow amazons.

Enjoy.

Nicole Kimberling
November 2008
Bellingham, Washington

Contents

Introduction	7
Raccoon Skin J.D. EveryHope	11
Amazons Jesse Sandoval	35
The Conclave Trent Roman	41
Under Suspicion Dr. Philip Edward Kaldon	63
Cupcake Erin MacKay	95
Dead and the President Tenea D. Johnson	139
About the Authors	176-177

Raccoon Skin

J.D. EveryHope

Sophia arrived at her parents' house just before dawn, jet-lagged from her red-eye flight. She let herself in, dropping her suitcases in the dining room and turning up the gas in the fireplace. Warm light flickered across the stark antiques. Her father had left the Bible open on the teak table and next to it, a half-finished cup of tea. Sophia brought the lukewarm cup into the cheerful kitchen and put it into the dishwasher.

She plucked a mint leaf from one of her mother's herb pots and chewed it as she made herself a latte. While she'd been away at college, her mother had put up another 'Viva Italia' poster. This one had about seventy types of pasta on it.

Outside, the trashcan was tipped over and coffee grounds, eggshells and styrofoam meat packaging were strewn across the white snow and the trashcan was tipped over. That tailless raccoon had gotten into the trash again. Sophia stepped out onto the patio. Snow crunched beneath her boots. She tipped the trashcan upright and swept up the meat packaging with the plastic broom that lived near the trash. Then she wrapped a bungee cord around the lid.

Daylight glowed, blue and pale, through the shadowed forest. A sharp wind clattered through the naked tree branches, and there was the sound of bird wings in the air. Dozens of crows, cawing, clustered around an eagle. The beautiful, beleaguered eagle dropped down and crashed into a snow drift. Crows dove down on it, and the injured eagle flopped in the snow.

Sophia grabbed the plastic broom and ran across her backyard. She whacked a crow. It skittered across the snow, stunned. The rest of the crows took flight, swirling above her. Still holding the broom, Sophia knelt next to the bleeding eagle. It cheeped at her, turning its head.

"Poor thing," she said. She didn't know if she could move it inside. It was pretty big and probably pretty angry. But she couldn't leave it outside while she called the animal rescue center, either, or the crows would come back.

The golden eagle shivered. In a flurry of light, feathers dropped from the bird. Bones shifted and flesh stretched into a familiar shape. Caterina lay naked on the snow, her smooth belly and round breasts prickling with goosebumps. A dozen oozing wounds were slashed across her pale skin and blood seeped through the snow beneath her. Sophia leaned forward and touched her girlfriend's face, her lips.

Caterina pressed her head against Sophia's knees, and blinked. "I made it," she breathed. Her chestnut hair was matted with blood and her golden eyes were dazed. "I can't believe I made it."

Crows landed on the branches of a maple and watched them with glistening black eyes.

"You were a bird," Sophia said. "You were just a bird, and now you're a person again."

"I'm so sorry. I'm so, so sorry." Caterina began to tremble, but it may have been the cold. "I couldn't tell you. I didn't think you would believe me."

"Ah, that's, um, understandable." If Sophia hadn't seen it, she probably would've suggested that Caterina visit Health Services and make an appointment with a professional. Preferably one who would medicate her.

"You're freezing." Sophia ran her hand down her girlfriend's skin. "Let's get you inside, okay?"

"No." Caterina glanced at the now empty sky. "No one can know that I'm here."

"I'll bring you to the guest house then. My parents never go there." Sophia couldn't have explained the mysterious arrival of a naked young woman to her parents, anyway. Besides, she hadn't exactly told Caterina that her parents didn't know about them yet. She'd never really mentioned that she hadn't come out to anyone at home. It had been hard enough to tell her mother that she was a vegetarian now, but that she had a girlfriend? Her mother might understand, might appreciate that Caterina was from Italy, but her father? No, he never would.

It was really for the best that her college life and home life hadn't met.

Sophia helped Caterina up, wrapping her arm around her girlfriend's neat waist. Together, they made a cold journey across the field to fake-rustic cottage. Sophia got the spare key out from under a pot of dead rosemary and unlocked the door.

Caterina pulled away from Sophia and limped to the couch, leaving blotches of blood on the floor.

"Just a second." Sophia ran back to the house and fetched the first aid kit from the bathroom and a blanket from the linens closet. Sitting down on the table across from Caterina, she began to wipe off the cuts with alcohol cloths, trying to get the grit out. She had never done this for anyone else before.

Caterina brushed her fingers across Sophia's hair in a thank-you gesture but didn't speak. She didn't complain or flinch, even though Sophia knew the cuts probably stung.

"You aren't really from Italy, are you?" Sophia put the damp cloth next to its paper wrapper and began rubbing antibacterial cream on the cuts.

"No. But I've been there. It's very similar to home."

"Oh, great. You've been there. As if that's the same thing." Sophia snapped the lid shut. "You know, I think I would have rather thought you were insane than know that you can live a lie, day after day, and seem completely honest while you're doing it."

"I shouldn't have come here." Caterina stood and took three wobbly steps forward. She reached out to touch the wall, as if she was drunk. "Shit."

"Sit down." Sophia stood and guided Caterina back down onto the couch. Her girlfriend's pupils were the same size, at least, and Sophia couldn't see any swelling on her skull, but that didn't mean there wasn't a lump hidden beneath her hair. "How do you feel?"

"I have to go. I have to get back." Caterina tried to stand again. "My aunt will kill me unless I stop her."

"Your aunt?"

"I think she killed my parents. I haven't heard from them this last month, but I thought that they were busy and then when I went home, she said she was Acting Regent for my little brothers, but I couldn't find them. I look and looked and couldn't find them and my parents must have been dead, dead and I didn't even know it, I was worrying about exams when they were dead and my little brothers could be anywhere."

"You're not going back," Sophia said. "You have to go to the hospital. I think you've got a concussion."

"I can't leave them there!" Blood was staining the blankets. "That's what I can't do."

"You're not going," Sophia said. "I could go instead."

"But you don't know what you're dealing with. You don't know anything about my world, about magic." Caterina shook her head and looked woozy.

"Stay here. I'll be back in a minute." Sophia darted back in the house, thankful that her parents weren't awake. Her parents didn't even know she was home, yet. She lugged her suitcase back down the stairs. She hid it behind a heap of boxes in the garage and returned to the small cottage. Later, she'd just tell her parents that her plane had been delayed and that she hadn't wanted to call them and wake them up. That would work.

Caterina was waiting for her. Sophia didn't know if she was glad, or not. It would have been a lot simpler if Caterina had left, but there she was, waiting on the couch.

Sophia brushed her fingers across her girlfriend's shoulder and bent down to kiss her. Caterina parted her lips, but Sophia pulled away.

"Knock on my door and tell my parents that you're a friend of mine, that you were mugged..." Sophia shrugged. "They'll probably think the worst, but they are good people. They'll help you."

Caterina nodded and removed a large ring from her finger. It had a red stone and reminded Sophia of class rings, only Caterina said it was a family heirloom. "When the first dawn strikes my signet ring, it will open the path of white light. You must follow that path to the other side of the morning star. Please find my brothers."

Sophia took the ring from Caterina's hand.

"I'm sorry," Caterina said.

"It's almost dawn. I have to go." Sophia knew exactly where the sun would hit the ground when it crossed over the trees and the edge of her roof. She set the signet ring into the snow, wrapped her arms around herself, and shivered, waiting.

The tailless raccoon was sitting on the trashcan, pulling at the bungee cord and trying to unlatch it. When he saw her, he paused and chattered. Then he jumped off the trashcan and waddled up to her. He had a stale croissant in his hand-like paws, which he turned over and over and rubbed in the snow.

The sun rose. White light cleared the shadows, and struck the ruby signet ring. There was a flare of color that hung in the air, almost like the forgotten strains of a song. Then Sophia saw the path, a shimmering bridge of fog, arcing into the sky.

The raccoon dropped the croissant and looked at her. He stood up on his hind legs and spoke in a sharp voice.

"Well, I had no idea that you had a gate to Beyond. You certainly didn't strike me as the type."

Sophia stared at the raccoon; first, her girlfriend had transformed from a golden eagle, and next, her neighborhood pest could talk. Go with it, she told herself. There's nothing else to do. "I wasn't, really. I suppose I have extenuating circumstances."

"You'd have to," he said. "It can be a harsh place. After a wizard chopped my tail off—it's a long story, but rest assured it wasn't exactly my fault—I decided to stay here, even though it's rather lonely."

"Um, I have to get going." She gestured at the path of dissipating fog.

"You can't go like that!" The raccoon wrung his little paws and looked at her with doleful brown eyes. "You'll get caught in a moment. Humans so rarely venture Beyond that when they do, everyone comes to gawk at them. You've heard the stories—Jack and the Bean Stalk, Hansel and Gretel, Little Red Riding Hood. The minute you step on that path, you'll cause quite a stir. All sorts of folks will be asking you to kiss their princesses."

"I already kiss the princess," Sophia said. "I'm way ahead of them."

The raccoon hesitated. He looked away, licking his lips and wiggling his wet black nose. "Well…you could always. No. It's a silly idea. But it would be safer …"

"What?"

"You could—" he hesitated again, "borrow my skin. You'd have to be very careful with it. You'd have to promise me that you wouldn't damage it, that you'd take very good care of it. I've grown rather attached to it."

"Borrow your skin?"

"Not exactly borrow. Maybe I should say that it would be more like an exchange. You can't wear two skins at once, after all.

That would be like trying to have two names at the same time. Uncomfortable. And one of us, namely me, would be left frozen here in this snow. You'll have to take your skin off first, and then put mine on."

"Humans can't take off their skins." Sophia wasn't sure she wanted anyone else to wear it while she was gone. She was rather attached to being herself, as awkward as it sometimes was.

"Sure they can, and the less likely you are to be recognized, the more likely you are to succeed." The raccoon popped the bungee cord off the trashcan and rooted around inside of it. He pulled out a piece of broken glass and handed it to her.

"Here you are. Now go on. Make a little cut."

She handed the glass back to him. "I think you should go first."

"Scaredy cat," the raccoon muttered. But it took the glass and made a small cut just below its breastbone. It dug its fingers in and unzipped the cut, stepping out of its skin as if it was no more than a furry jumpsuit.

Sophia took a deep breath and made the cut. The raccoon instructed her on taking her skin off. She peeled her fingers off one by one like they were gloves. She pulled her face off by the back of her hair, and then wriggled out of her torso like she was taking off a too-tight sweater. Then she shimmied out of the rest her skin, and handed it over to the raccoon. She picked up his heavy furry hide, and stepped into it. It was sort of like trying to put on a pair of jeans about three sizes too small. She wiggled and twisted, and her boobs got stuck. When she had the raccoon skin on, she felt like her flesh was pinched at the seams.

It had been much easier for the raccoon to get into her skin. It looked like the tips of her fingers were a bit loose on him, and her legs were a bit floppy. But then he seemed to fill her skin and perhaps she shrank a little to fit his, because suddenly it didn't pinch so much.

"Well, thanks," Sophia said. "I have to go—and, don't hurt it, okay!"

"I won't!" the raccoon called after her.

Sophia started climbing the path. Her legs sunk into the fog at first, but then she got the hang of walking on it. She walked all the way over the horizon and her world disappeared in a bluish haze behind her. She was in Beyond, now, wherever that was. Shapes started to coalesce from the mist around her and the shining path hardened into glazed bricks. The road she was walking on crossed a hilly valley, hemmed in by bluish peaks. Trees with silvered leaves snapped in the breeze and brown moths flickered in front of her, like the brush of cobwebs. The forest opened into abandoned cornfields, where vines of zucchini and squash sprawled across the ground and small peas curled up the corn stalks, sporting white and pink flowers.

The village may have been termed "sleepy" if there had been a single sound. But there wasn't a whisper of a breeze, no sound of crickets or even a hen clucking. Sophia adjusted the skin where it was bunching around her stomach. She encountered a rather large pocket, the same sort one found on large sweatshirts, and she dipped her hands in.

Something squished, and she dug out several old orange peels, a chicken bone, and dropped the other half of the raccoon's stale croissant on the ground. She also found a pair of her mother's broken Gucci sunglasses, a small stuffed tiger that she thought she'd lost years ago, and one of her broken makeup compacts.

Sophia tucked the sunglasses into her pocket. She held the stuffed tiger between her hands and gazed into its black bead eyes, and then wiggled the paws back and forth with her fingers. "Hello, Blaze. I thought I'd lost you at my eighth birthday party, but you've been around all along, haven't you? That'd be just like you."

Blaze the Tiger shivered in her hands. Startled, she dropped the worn stuffed animal onto the glazed brick. Before her eyes, the stuffed animal turned into turned into the familiar shape she had imagined so many times. She had spent hours and hours beneath the front porch with her arm wrapped over the shoulders of her tiger, watching the driveway and waiting for her father to come home. Sophia dropped to her knees and pressed her face into the rough orange fur of Blaze's neck and breathed in. Blaze still smelled like a stuffed animal.

Sophia flipped open the compact and looked into the mirror. She saw herself. She didn't look like a raccoon, despite the skin she wore. Behind her the land was ruined, desolate. Instead of a deserted village, she saw a burnt-out wreck where only the tumbledown chimneys stood. Instead of softly shushing corn, she saw broken stalks and rotted zucchini. The forest behind her was withered and the tips of the trees were sheathed with a writhing brown mass of tent caterpillars.

Sophia looked at Blaze with the mirror and it showed her only the stuffed animal with black button eyes. She snapped it shut.

So, the mirror showed the truth, then. It showed how things really were. If the land was this desolate, Caterina's aunt was probably just as terrible as Caterina had said. Her girlfriend's family was in danger.

Blaze took Sophia's hand in her mouth and tugged. Sophia let Blaze pull her out of the ruined village and along the shining road. A blue star, perhaps it was the morning star, hung directly above the road near the crescent moon. A flurry of moths descended on her and she brushed them out of her face.

She passed over a hill, and in front of her, the shining road had crumbled. A deep chasm broke it, dark stone with small trees growing from the cracks in the rock.

Raccoon Skin

"Oh no." Sophia looked at Blaze. "This has got to be some sort of joke."

When she'd been little, she'd had this dream again and again. She'd stood on the edge of the chasm and slipped, clawing at the crumbling sides, and then right before she hit the ground, she'd woken up. She'd never been able to make herself to go to sleep after that and had wandered the house in the dark, listening to her father snoring, playing with her toys. The silence hadn't been much different from the daytime.

Sophia grabbed the compact from the raccoon's pockets, and looked at the chasm in the mirror. It showed only the shining road, which continued uninterrupted.

Swallowing, she stepped into emptiness. It was solid beneath her. So she just tried not to look down.

Above her, crows circled.

Sophia hunched and got to the other side. Moths crawled across her skin, tangled in her hair. Sophia picked them out, and she walked beneath the blue morning star until it was behind her.

The crows were definitely watching her. Were they people, like her girlfriend or the raccoon? Were they spying on her?

Clusters of dark rotting branches closed in over the shining path. Ahead, the path was blocked with branches and a very large tree stump. Sophia grabbed a handful of the bark and tried to pull herself over, but it crumbled into dust. Blaze bumped into her and purred.

Once upon a time, Sophia had imagined Blaze just like this. She had spoken to Blaze, mimicking her Italian mother's language, unable to really say anything at all. She had played beneath the kitchen table, breathing in the scent of pasta, il formaggio, and fresh garlic. Her mother used to sing *Volare* and Sophia still knew the words. She had pretended that she was riding Blaze all across the jungle, defeating pythons, gorillas, and men with turbans.

Now Sophia climbed onto Blaze's back, like she had so many times before in her mind, and Blaze's purr rumbled beneath her. Blaze leapt up, and Sophia had to dig her fingers into the warm ruff of fur. Blaze latched her claws into the large tree stump and clambered up. The stump began to crumble beneath their combined weight, and Blaze leapt clear. They continued along the path.

Sophia walked until her feet hurt. She sat on the cobbled road and leaned against Blaze. Sophia looked up into the eerie sky. The full moon hung behind her like a ripe honeydew melon, but barely visible between the flickering bodies of crows. Hunger burned in her stomach and she absently picked up one of the grubs inching across the road and ate it. It burst between her teeth like a stem of rotten spinach. She knew that she should've minded it, but didn't. Perhaps it was the raccoon skin. Sophia slept against Blaze. She woke, walked and slept again.

She was sure that time was passing, but the sky was unchanging. The only other way she had to gauge time was her own weariness and her stomach, and her stomach had become a stranger in her own body. She only hoped that she wasn't too late, that Caterina's little brothers were still alive, that she hadn't failed Caterina.

Over yet another hill, she came to a place that was almost a town, as close to a town as she'd seen in this strange rural land, anyway. The crumbled buildings were made from brick, and some were even two stories high, the balconies draped with desiccated plants.

A sharp scream pierced the air. Sophia jumped, and looked around. No one was there. Then she saw a flash of movement beyond. Muffled sobbing burst into the emptiness.

A girl, about Sophia's age, crouched in the ruins of a building, clutching her ankle. Her dress was the dusty gray of last year's cobwebs and hung in tatters over her slender frame.

"Please, you have to help me. It's stuck."

Sophia stepped forward.

Blaze got in front of her, and growled.

"Please, please, something is chasing me. I don't know what it is, but I'm the last one left!" The girl stepped forward, trying to pull her ankle out, an expression of pain pinching her pretty face. "It's going to get me, just like it got all of the others!"

She knew it had to be a trap, but Sophia couldn't help herself. She couldn't stay on the path when that girl was helpless and caught. She stepped around Blaze. The moment her foot touched the dirt, the girl's face dissolved into wriggling worms and her body lurched toward Sophia, a writhing mass of caterpillars. Blaze leapt forward, pouncing on the creature. The caterpillars squirmed across the ground, mashed to jelly by Blaze's huge weight.

Sophia ran toward Blaze, but by the time she got there, it was too late. Worms wriggled inside Blaze's stuffing and her button eyes dropped from their threads, caterpillars protruding from the stitching. Sophia knelt, clutching the stuffed animal to her. But Blaze was dead, the worn plush cold against her face. Sophia clawed the worms out of the stuffing, throwing them, stomping on their pulpy bodies. Sophia fought not to cry, not to cry over this little stuffed animal. A sob was caught in her throat, something like the coughing grunt a tiger makes. Sophia swallowed and rubbed at her dry eyes.

The infested forest rose and above her, the dark bare branches were wreathed with webs and the sky was blocked with masses of caterpillars. Moths crawled across Sophia's skin. Soft popping sounds filled the air, like rice crispies, the sound of a thousand mandibles working. The shining path was nowhere to be seen.

Wriggling caterpillars dropped from the trees, trying to burrow into her hair. Sophia flung the caterpillars off her broken Blaze—threw their sticky little feet, their padded fatty lengths, down into the dirt. She put the stuffed animal in the raccoon skin pocket and stepped forward, feeling rubbery caterpillars beneath her feet.

Now she didn't even have Blaze for company. "If someone else was here, if anyone else was here, they'd know the right direction." Sophia continued walking, mostly because she didn't want to stay where she was. The forest grew darker, the pale nests of wriggling caterpillars blotting out branches and sky. The light could barely seep through and she forgot to notice the feeling of caterpillars crawling across her skin.

Then a crow burst through the nests, startling her. A shard of sunlight fell through the branches onto the dirt floor. The crow hopped along a branch and pecked at a caterpillar, then preened some of the filmy debris from his dark feathers. Then, sure that he had got her attention, the crow fluttered to another branch and cawed.

"You can't want me to follow you. You tried to kill Caterina," Sophia told it.

The crow stared down at her, swinging its head back and forth, looking at her with one eye and then the other.

"Why won't you answer?" she cried, squeezing the stuffed animal in her pocket. "Why won't you talk to me?"

The crow hopped to the next branch.

Sophia didn't know what to do, but the crow was alive and looking at her. That was the only reason she had to follow it, but it was enough of a reason for her. The crow cackled and hopped into the air. Sophia dashed forward to the tree, gazing at the obscured sky.

"Wait! Don't leave yet. Not yet. Please don't leave," she said, putting her hand on the tree trunk.

Sophia turned and walked right into a wall. She blinked, and rubbed her nose. A dab of blood smeared across her fingers, and her nose stung. The caterpillars went crazy, wiggling across her skin with their sticky feet, clustering around the blood. She shook them off, and ran along the wall. The caterpillars were dropping from the trees, plop, plop, plop, carpeting the ground with their velvety flesh. They squished beneath her feet, releasing squelching goo. She darted through a gap in the wall and found herself in a courtyard.

This must be the palace.

She walked through the stained marble halls, echoingly empty, and looked out of the arched windows that revealed nothing but a barren wilderness, writhing with insects. The halls became bigger, and she almost felt like a virus traversing the veins of a quiescent monster. The great hall was an expansive space, ribbed arches vaulting into a distant dark ceiling. The windows were sealed up with blackened curtains, and out of the many candelabras lining the long and empty hall, only three short, stuttering candles were lit. The rest seemed to have melted down and not been replenished. Wax stalagmites dotted the marble floor.

Sophia heard her footsteps resound. It felt like she was striking a bell. As she moved deeper into the cavernous space, she could sense movement in front of her, almost feel it.

Then a torch flared to life, right in front of her.

"Welcome." A mature woman sat on the throne. Her body was corseted with a form-fitting dress and her dark hair caught on the beaded silks like webbing. The throne shimmered golden with the light on the flame, and Sophia could see a small bird's nest perched in the jeweled tines. Two adolescent crows poked their heads out, all purplish pin-feathers, and croaked. Hundreds of crows, robins, wrens, and other birds in wooden cages hung from the ceiling. They croaked and beat themselves against the bars that imprisoned them. Chains rattled, and the cages bumped into long draping nets filled with raw eyes. Some of the eyes burst, and pale fluid dripped to the floor.

"Who are you?" Sophia asked, swallowing back her fear.

"I am called The Mother of Thousands and you have seen my sons and daughters populating my land and the forests surrounding the palace," the woman said, "but I think you want me to tell you that I am Caterina's aunt."

One of the baby crows tumbled out of the nest and croaked piteously. The woman's black eyes flickered to it, and then away.

"I'm not trying to kill Caterina," the woman said. "I'm only trying to bring her home."

The baby crow struggled across the floor, flapping its partially developed wings and hopping. It bumped into Sophia's foot.

"I am first-born, as Caterina is first-born. I can change shape, as she does, and am very magically gifted. I was a strong and wise young woman and I studied with the most preeminent sorcerers, acquiring knowledge and learning about the common folk. I cared for my land."

"So what?" Sophia asked, kneeling so that she could nudge the baby crow away. She didn't want to step on it or anything. But as soon as her hand was near the crow, it pecked her. Sort of. She saw that it had left a small silver screw in her hand, like the kind that fit into glasses.

"I could not inherit, just as Caterina will not inherit. Despite her strength, kindness, confidence and wisdom, she will never inherit the throne. She will have to watch, as I have watched, when her brothers ruin this once strong and beautiful land. I have watched it wither beneath my brother's rule and I have mourned its pathetic stagnation."

Sophia stood and stuck her hands in her pockets. She felt her mother's broken sunglasses in there, and absently she began to fiddle with the screw. It slid into place, wedging the frame around the lens.

"I don't really know anything about this," Sophia said, trying to keep Caterina's aunt talking until she could figure out what to do.

"Is it just that only men can inherit this land? No matter what I did to prove my competence, I could not change the rules of this land."

"That doesn't seem right," Sophia said. She wondered if Caterina wanted this inheritance. They'd never been able to talk about it before, really. She wondered what it would be like if they stayed together, and Sophia had to come to this place where women were considered inferior. Their relationship probably wouldn't be acceptable. Would they be able to live like that?

She slid the sunglasses on. Through one lens she saw Caterina's aunt as her own mother might, self-pitying, ugly, vindictive.

Then she shook her head at the ridiculousness of it. She was wearing a raccoon skin and a pair of broken sunglasses in a decrepit fairyland. She had no way to get home, to see if Caterina was alright. Besides, she had real life-threatening problems to deal with and she didn't want to deal with this woman's private melodrama.

"It isn't right," Caterina's aunt said, mostly to herself. "I was better. I was the best."

"You know," Sophia said, "if this is an example of a kingdom under your control, then that just proves you aren't fit to rule."

The woman opened up her hands in a gesture of amused helplessness.

"Did you kill Caterina's parents when you seized the throne? Did you hurt her little brothers?"

The woman laughed. "Oh no, but I can. I can hurt them if you should refuse me. How do you think Caterina will take it, their blood on your hands?"

"Not on my hands." Sophia grabbed the torch, and thrust it against a hanging sack of eyes. The eyes caught fire, hissing and spitting as they split open, and rolling along the floor as the net burnt through. The fire leapt from net to net, and more dark furry caterpillars crawled from the burst open eyes, writhing in the boiling juices.

The woman hissed, and her human shape melted away into a large, undulating grub, and moths burst out from her porous skin.

Ashes drifted down from the rafters, and the crows were everywhere, hopping along the floor with clipped wings. Some could fly and flapped into the air, circling and cawing. The large caterpillar had disappeared, and now Sophia could only see the flock of crows.

She fumbled through her raccoon suit to pull something out, to get something. Sophia found the mirror that showed the truth and stared into it, trying to see through the dark heavy smoke, ash, and the changing light of the flames.

Then she saw it. The crows, the birds, were all people. Caterina's aunt hid among them. Her face was nervous, drawn tight with panic, but it was unmistakably her beneath the shadow of a crow's shape.

Sophia couldn't believe that she was doing this, not even a little. But she grabbed the bird—now it was a dog snapping at her hands, now it was a bear, now a tender-looking kitten—and she held the woman against the flames. The woman's shape flickered into a caterpillar as she writhed, her flesh popping and deflating in the flame.

Sickened, Sophia shoved the vile body away and sank to her knees. She buried her face in her hands and glad for once that she'd been alone.

Someone touched her shoulder, a hand that felt very human, small and slightly damp with sweat. Sophia blinked, rubbed her eyes, and looked around.

Subjects and servants dressed in strange and gravity-defying costumes of blue, green and orange lined the walls where the birds had once been. All at once they began to chat and laugh. Some danced across the throne room, leaving flowers in their footprints. Fauns brought out flutes for the fairy choirs, and a chorus of bullfrogs had a singing contest with the pixies who rode across the budding branches on curl-shell snails. Leaves burst into color as Sophia watched. The few birds that remained played games of tag with ribbons in their claws.

Two little boys stood next to her, very nervous. They were obviously Caterina's little brothers, because they shared her sharp facial features and her dramatic golden coloring. Their pale chestnut hair was singed very badly, and stood up in small tufts. Sophia could not help but smile at them.

"Hello," the older boy said. "My name is Francis and this is my little brother Sam. Who are you?"

"My name is Sophia and I…know your sister," she finished lamely. Overwhelmed in the fashion of an only child faced with kids, she stood up. "Where are your parents?"

"I am here," the king said. He was a strong-looking man with thin lips and a sharp nose. His wife stood near him—she looked like she maybe came from a different part of the country, because with her dark hair and pale skin she looked very unlike her children and husband. She smiled a little and took the king's hand. They both managed to look quite regal, despite their state of undress and the fact that they were covered in soot. Servants rushed up, covering them in garments of feathers and rubies.

Maybe this happened often around here.

"I am very pleased to meet you and proud that my daughter sent such a … wise young woman to our aid," said the king. "Now, tell me what you would like as your reward? A room full of gold, a garment of starlight, a dove that will sort out lentils? If it is within my power to grant, you will have it."

"Could you declare Caterina your heir?" Sophia asked.

The throne room went quiet. The fauns lowered their flutes, the bullfrogs clapped their mouths shut, and the pixies gave quiet squeaks of dismay and clung to each other. The king looked down at Sophia with his face proud and stern. Sophia was crouched in front of him in her raccoon skin suit and she felt suddenly like vermin that had intruded upon the king's joy.

But she waited, anyway.

"So be it," the king said.

"Thank you," Sophia said.

"Where is Caterina anyway?" Sam asked, grabbing her hand. His huge red pantaloons flared around his feet.

"Caterina is staying with my family right now," Sophia said. "If it pleases you, I'd like to go home soon."

"You may leave our presence," the king said.

"But I lost the shining road on the way here, so I don't know if I can get back the way I came." Sophia wrung her tiny black hands together.

"Of course you can't," the queen said. "No one ever walks the same path twice! Let us conduct you home so that we may thank your parents in person."

So it was that Sophia departed. The king and the queen scattered cherry blossoms into the first beam of moonlight they found and Sophia stepped into her world. Her girlfriend's family followed her, stepping into the meadow behind Sophia's house just as the moon glinted through the trees. They were still dressed pretty archaically. Perhaps she could pass them off as historical reenactors. But first, she had to get out of her raccoon skin suit.

She led Caterina's parents to her front door, then scrambled down the stairs as they knocked.

Her mother answered. "Hello. Is there anything I can help you with?"

"Yes. We're Caterina's parents," the king said. "Sophia called us."

"Oh, I see. Please come in," her mother said.

Sophia circled around the house, climbing up the back steps to the patio. She pushed open the glass doors.

"Hey, knock that off!"

The raccoon started and looked at her, his dark beady eyes shining out from her face. He leaned over the refrigerator, going through the produce drawer and throwing green, red and yellow bell peppers on the floor. Flour and pasta were already scattered all across the floor, along with scattered broken dishes, half-eaten slices of bread, prosciutto, parmesan, as well as several tomatoes. A half-gallon carton of milk was tilted on its side and slowly glugging onto the tile floor.

"I'd like my skin back now," she said.

The raccoon sighed and began sliding it off. "I wasn't even done with the fridge, yet, and I hadn't investigated all the shiny things. You could've taken longer, you know. You really could've," he complained.

She set her stuffed Blaze on the counter. That was one thing she had found she was not willing to give back to the raccoon. "If I find anything missing, anything at all—" Sophia began, holding the raccoon's skin back out to him.

"Ye-es," the raccoon said, looking sideways. "Nothing's missing. Nope, no, no. You'll see." He grabbed his skin and tossed hers back to her. They both got dressed, not looking at each other's bare muscles.

"Aw," the raccoon said, combing through his fur with his small paws and teeth. "You stretched it out. I supposed you couldn't help it, but it will take days to get it to fit properly again."

"Sophia!" her mother called. "What are you doing up there?"

"Yikes!" The raccoon laughed and scooted out the kitchen. He scampered out onto the patio, chittered at her, and dashed across the yard and into the woods.

"What happened in here?" her mother asked, coming up the stairs.

"Raccoons? I'm trying to clean up?" Sophia stretched her hands, trying to make sure her skin was fitting correctly. Her left knuckle felt baggy, and she wondered what the raccoon had done to her finger.

Her mother picked up the leaking milk carton and set it on the counter. "You've been acting a little off all day today. Are you sure you're all right?"

"Yes," Sophia said.

Her mother sighed a little, but said nothing. Sophia began washing vegetables and putting them back into the produce drawer.

"Your friend seems very nice." Her mother said, pulled the broom out of the closet and began sweeping the flour into a tidy pile. "It's terrible, what happened to her. How did you meet her?"

"In the residence hall cafeteria. She couldn't figure out how the microwave worked." Sophia smiled. She had also spent hours teaching Caterina how to use computers and secretly wondering if there were communities of the Amish in Italy all the while. But at the time it had seemed like a good opportunity to spend time with a beautiful girl.

"Well, I'm glad that her parents got here so soon," her mother said, maneuvering the flour into a dust pan. "She's really going to need all of the emotional support they can provide. She keeps on saying that she just fell, but I don't know…"

"If that's what she says, then you had better let it rest." Sophia wiped up the last of mess on the kitchen floor with a couple of towels. "We need some antiraccoon spray or something. This is ridiculous."

Her mother laughed. "At the garden shop one of the clerks recommended a spray made out of coyote urine. I think we must've accumulated a whole family of raccoons. You should let me finish up here so you can talk to your friend."

"Thanks." Sophia kissed her mother on the cheek. Would explaining that Caterina was more than "just a friend" heal or break her relationship with her parents? Was taking the chance worth it?

Well, she was going to see. At the worst, she'd be on her own and she knew that many of her friends were doing that, relying on loans and working. It wouldn't be fun, but she could do that. She had to give her parents a chance to get to know who she really was.

"Hey, I'll tell you what's going on in my life sometime. I just don't know if I'm ready yet."

"Whenever you're ready," her mother said, and Sophia knew she'd done the right thing.

In the living room, Caterina was sitting on the couch, reading and drinking hot chocolate while her family had gathered around the TV. Her youngest brother, Sam poked at the buttons curiously, turning the TV on and off, on and off. Caterina glanced up from her book of Grimm's Fairytales when Sophia came in through the door.

"I'm so glad you're back," she whispered. "That raccoon you left here was a handful. I had to watch him like a hawk."

"Or an eagle?" Sophia suggested.

Caterina smiled, shy.

Sophia sat down next to her, and leaned her head on her shoulder and breathed in her scent, something clean and sweet like a honeydew melon. "You're feeling better, right?" she asked.

"Yes. The doctors gave me a CAT scan and said that they couldn't find any bleeding in my brain," Caterina said. "I still can't believe, well, they're here, aren't they? You did it. You are amazing, surely amazing." A small smile curved Caterina's lips and Sophia could see that she was so happy her golden eyes nearly glowed.

How often had Caterina sat in a dreary lecture hall and been homesick, but never mentioned it simply because she couldn't?

Sophia looked to see if Caterina's family was watching, but they remained enthralled by the TV. Sam had found the button that controlled the channels, and he poked it repeatedly, switching between CNN and Japanese game show where the contestants had to swim across a pool of banana pudding.

"It's magic," Sam cried.

Sophia kissed Caterina and said, "We're going to be just fine."

Amazons

Jesse Sandoval

The waters split themselves across my oar. They sweep over its smooth wood as if they were caressing it. They toss themselves up and tease its expanse promising that the river is filled with nothing but whores. A foot away I can see the yellow gaze of a crocodile, its long form lingering just under the muddy surface. Draped across the overhanging branches, black snakes cool their glistening bodies. They lie in wait for the naïve or curious to stare too long into the rippling current. Then they drop their coils around fools' throats.

Once I saw one of those snakes lift a grown man off his feet and swallow him whole. The man pissed himself as the snake wrapped herself around him as if she were falling in love. She opened her thin mouth and took him in a deep kiss. I watched her eyes the entire time. She had the mesmerized gaze of utter adoration, as if this man's form, his meat and muscle, had entranced her and drawn her into an unthinkable action.

I remember seeing that same unflinching stare long ago, looking back at me from a silver mirror. My hands trembled as I tried to load the pistol, the slender bullets wavered and slipped between my fingers. Then I caught sight of myself in a mirror. I gazed into my own eyes, the wide pupils dilated, entranced with desire. My reflection knew that I was a murderess before I did. She passed that assurance to me in a glance. My fingers have never trembled since.

But that was before I came to the river and she opened her warm body to my motions. Years before, when I would sit at my

Aunt Sofia's cherry wood table, with a delicate teacup pinched between my gloved fingers. All of my aspirations circulated inside those china cups, dissipating like steam before they reached my lips.

I longed secretly—so secretly that not even I knew it. Only the silent night-motions of my dreams knew and they spoke only to the mirror on my dressing table. Night after night I turned and twisted, whispered and rolled as if possessed. Every morning I woke innocently twisted in the bondage of my white linens. Then I would rise and the rest of my day would pour forth in polite servings of milky tea. In small sips taken from tiny china cups.

I never liked the desolate paleness of white until I saw Maria. She was dancing, swirling and spinning, turning her white gown silver with her movements. Her perfect body swung and shone like a hypnotist's pendulum. I swayed and stared, my gaze unable to pull away from her. My every thought moved to her, attending her motions, and hearing only the whispers of her silk gown.

We shared slices of cake and sipped lemonade and we spoke of things unknown. We told each other tales of the New World, laughing over those foolish monsters with unbalanced limbs and telescopic eyes. Sloths and chameleons. We talked as if the Americas and Australia, India and New Guinea were our personal gardens. As if they were not countries, but stories that we had made up for each other's pleasure. She offered me islands of blue fires and blind fish as clear as glass. I told her about the mountains of Chile where vast clouds of gold and violet butterflies hid the sun when they took flight. Their beating wings sounded like thunder. When we turned our conversation home we came arm in arm like jaded travelers mistakenly dressed in debutante gowns.

Maria said she detested all the cheeses of France and Spain. They were nothing but infested curds of rotted cream. Nothing compared to the coconut nectar that I had fed her in the scarlet mountains. I decided the Eiffel tower was now unbearably ugly, more trash heap than monument, next to the vast weavings of Maria's jewel spiders.

We gave each other gifts that no suitor could match, secrets that no other could know and visions only we could share. All of it in utter innocence. But that means nothing.

The black snake in the branches is innocent as the Virgin, it makes no difference to the man digesting in her coils. Full of innocence, we had no name for our passion and no fear of what we could do or what would come.

We sat close, hardly sparing a glance for my suitors or her husband. We spent days that way. When Robert came for her he always frowned at me. He seemed puzzled, as if he could not see anything in Maria that would so entrance me.

He looked at her and saw something smaller than himself, something not quite as alive. She was a trophy to him, a fragile creature that he had captured.

"My pet," he called her. "Ah there's my little bird," he would say, as if his words could capture her in the brass cage beside his bed. It was the same cage that we smashed to pieces, while he was away on safari.

"My butterfly," he would say as he claimed her hand for a dance. "My flower," he would whisper after. His words, his motions, every elegant expression was a weight he worked down on her, as if she were a violet to be pressed.

"Soon I'll be no more than baby's breath," Maria told me. "He thinks he loves me but all he does is quash me…"

When Robert returned from hunting he was always surprised to find his house suffused with jasmine perfume and feral cats. The furniture had been knocked aside as if wild animals had been loosed in the drawing room. His bedding had been torn to strips and sails, for the great ships Maria and I would ride together.

The first time we kissed Maria left the taste of jasmine on my lips. It was a scent and a taste that was only hers. I have never known a blossom to smell so singular and clean. Even now I think the flowers are a poor imitation.

On the river the perfumes are dark and so ripe that they are half-rotten. The smell is more intoxicating and decadent than the court of the Sun King could ever have been. Succulent flowers, sweet mangos and slick pools of golden urine tint the humid air, clinging to my skin. Beads of condensation and sweat glitter through my hair and drip into the flowing water.

Life here is unrestrained and unashamed. Lush orchids, with petals like wet silk and curling velvet, grow up through piles of antelope shit without apology. Their bodies as long as my forearm and greener than emeralds, the mantis women fuck their men then devour them with the shameless ease of nature.

And the great river pours herself out like a ceaseless hunger, swallowing men and beasts, machines and soil in her passionate body. She takes any man who comes to her, not as so many believe to ease his lonely heart. No, she takes them like a Mantis Queen, like the black snakes, like a flood that swallows endlessly because that is what it is.

I know this because I know her. I push my pole and my narrow boat against her surface like a needle sliding into a vein. I am a mosquito in an opium den, drunk on the blood of this woman. I know her currents and her curves because they have filled my body and fed me so long. She suffuses the thick air and sinks into the soil. She feeds the fruit with her rich juice. As we drink from her, she swallows us, overflowing our blood and flesh, flooding our dreams and drawing us in.

She was in my heart when Maria and I read together, leaning close over the stories of undefeatable forests and all their wild beasts.

Maria's perfume and breath filled my lungs, tasting better than common air. Her presence was my atmosphere, her body the only home I longed for. She looked into my eyes and her image ignited like silver nitrate. She burned into me.

I told her that I loved her as we sat by the cropped lawn watching Robert and the other gentlemen play.

"How could you?" she asked. "I'm just another woman. There is nothing new in me."

"You are an entire world in your own right. The silver webs of the jewel spiders and red rivers and the weeping lilies, you are all of those."

"But those are only stories."

"But they are your stories, and yours alone. All those places exist only within you. You are an Atlantis and the Seven Cities of Gold. You are a treasure that cannot be equaled, a new world that has made this home of my own tepid and dull. I would leave it all for you," I told her.

"Would you?" She pressed her hands to her breasts as if in prayer and then slowly folded my hands in her own, imparting that caress to my fingers.

"I would do anything." My words were not loud. They were the beats of a butterfly's wings summoning thunder. We both felt it roll over us like a premonition.

I had never known what I was until that moment. Aunt Sofia had always said that I was a spring violet and all the world was my rainstorm. But she was only looking into my eyes and seeing her own reflection. She had only been talking to herself over teacups all those years.

"She was afraid of the truth," Maria said, "because you are not her niece. You are a stolen child from the wilds within me. You have come to set me free."

I nodded, and the truth of what she said opened up inside me like the jaws of a venus flytrap. That night I met my own gaze in the mirror for the first time. I was wide-eyed and innocent as an adder.

Robert, of all people, should have recognized that. He had hunted wolves on the Russian ice and foxes through the remains of England. He was not cruel, perhaps. But he did not love Maria. Not as I did. Not enough to be transformed by her and not enough to give her freedom.

And now, on the river, I meet the yellow eyes of a crocodile as she glides past and I return her pressed smile. Below the waters she has a cache of pigs and fishermen's limbs. In the belly of my boat bundles of iridescent green iguana skins are tucked next to three crocodile hides. She dives and I push on across the water.

Death is not justice; it is a consequence. It comes when a man misses the motions of a snake, when he does not see the bright, wide gaze of love for what it is. Robert did not deserve to die any more than an antelope deserves the jaws of a crocodile. He simply did not understand my smile that night when he came to take Maria and my bullet found his heart. It was not a moral question. We both wanted her, but Maria handed the gun to me.

Now the waters swell, and I stroke them and ride their motions to their source. Maria is there, between the long green shadows and the piercing shafts of light. Her wild hair flows with sweet jasmine blooms. She is laughing and thinking of the stories that she will whisper against my lips tonight. Her waters swirl and arch as she brings me in.

The Conclave

Trent Roman

In Tanya Drake's opinion, the hardest part about going steady with someone several millennia older than herself was probably the pillow talk. Erin wasn't the most down-to-earth person under any circumstances but her feckless sense of timing always seemed to worsen after sex. Tanya would be enjoying the moment after *the* moment, and Erin had to go and ruin it by bringing up past lovers. This was always a horrible *faux pas* regardless of one's background. But the names in Erin's mental black book reached back centuries and included such daunting figures as Sappho herself.

Tanya by no means considered herself a prude. In most other relationships, she would be considered the troublemaker. But there was something about the afterglow of sex that had always verged on the sacred. So it was rather unwelcome to hear, while trying to bask in that post-orgasmic glow, Erin's voice saying, "Oh, FYI, that trick I just did with the tongue? Picked it up from one of Genghis Khan's concubines."

Tanya would simply lie there, silent, wondering how the hell she was supposed to reply to a comment like that. "Hey, thanks for sharing. Please, continue to regale me with tales of your sexual exploits with medieval Mongolian women."

Erin's assortment of personal quirks were as unique as Erin herself: the way she would sometimes smile, unprovoked and faintly contemptuous, as though making a private joke at Tanya's expense, or how she would grow and retract her hair and fingernails when she was bored, as though hoping somebody would notice and freak out.

Tanya had met Erin at a private Catholic school in the immigrant district of Chasm City informally referred to as the East 'Shrooms, a dumping ground for the city's 'undesirable Europeans' in years past. It was one of those schools whose administrators insisted on making its female students wear the pleated skirt, white shirt and dark tie combo, despite its near iconic embodiment of the schoolgirl fetish.

Erin had been leaning against a brick wall just across the street from the school, one leg folded backwards with her foot against the wall as though striking a pose—which, in retrospect, she probably was. From the wild red curls reaching down to the middle of her back, the freckles across her fair face, and the uniform she wore, Tanya assumed that she was just another transplanted child of Old Éire serving out her sentence until college and freedom. It was a chilly April day, but Erin wasn't wearing a coat over her shirt—and, quite visibly given the cold, wasn't wearing a bra underneath it either.

At that point, Tanya was several months removed from a bad break up with a girl who had decided, after much 'explaining' by her father, priest and other assorted meddlers, that she wasn't gay after all, and so Tanya wasn't really looking to start another thing. It was Erin who called out as Tanya was passing by. According to her, the *sidhe* had perfected 'gaydar' over the millennia until they could read a person's preferences like a flashing neon billboard. Tanya, gladdened by the seeming coincidence, accepted Erin's proposition to join her at the local discotheque later that night.

It wasn't long before Erin's physical charms and devil-may-care attitude had led them to Tanya's bedroom. Just six hours, in fact. Erin had claimed that her place wasn't amenable to that kind of activity, but Tanya lived alone with her father, a kind if somewhat hapless man who had some time ago decided against asking about Tanya's one-on-one 'slumber parties' with other girls. According to him, Tanya's mother, whom she had no memory of, was on a fifteen-year mission in the Caribbean, spreading the Word. Tanya suspected that mommy dearest was on a fifteen-year fling with some beach boy named Raoul. Such things were not spoken of in that domicile: their own 'don't ask, don't tell' policy.

A few weeks into their whirlwind affair, as they rested on Tanya's bed in postcoital bliss, Erin casually mentioned that she was actually a *sidhe*. Tanya, thinking it some new game, had challenged Erin to a demonstration of her otherworldly powers.

"How about a glamour?" Erin said. "Look down."

Tanya did so, and to her horror discovered that she had suddenly acquired extra (and gender-inappropriate) equipment lower down. With a startled shriek she tried to scurry away from it, but naturally the fat member remained attached, merely flopping about as Tanya fell over the side of the bed. With a twinkling laugh, Erin dispelled the illusion.

"Please don't ever do that again," Tanya said at length, feeling to make sure her body had been restored to its original design.

After getting over the initial shock, Tanya pumped Erin for as much information on fairies as her enigmatic girlfriend would reveal. When Erin mentioned that she was old enough to have witnessed the Pyramids being built, Tanya had good-naturedly accused her inamorata of being a pedophile, hanging out in schoolyards, looking to pick up impressionable young women.

"Girl," Erin had said, "when you date people who measure their lifespan in mere decades, any relationship is robbing the cradle. A few decades here or there doesn't make difference. Also, building the Pyramids? A lot more boring than most people think. Whip, grunt, pull. Whip, grunt, pull. Some of the other fairies might go for the whole sweaty men in loincloths scenario, but it's not really my thing, you know?"

In fact, there was much Tanya didn't know about Erin, and after a few weeks, it started to get on her nerves. She never wanted to be 'that type' of girlfriend, suspicious and possessive, but Erin's tendency to vanish for days only to reappear expecting to pick up where they had left off as though no time had passed quickly lost its roguish appeal. Tanya's frustration with Erin's inconsistent presence magnified those other irritants—the constant reminders that she was the less experienced partner, the amused sense of superiority Erin sometimes projected, and yes, even the pillow-talk (although Tanya would never admit it out loud-it sounded petty just thinking about it).

One day when returning home from school, she caught sight of Erin across the street, crouching and holding a conversation with a fire hydrant. Traffic was too heavy to cross, but Tanya called out. Erin, turned her head, saw her, and flashed a toothy smile. A large truck momentarily blocked Tanya's line of sight, and when it passed, Erin was gone.

Tanya was only mildly surprised to find Erin waiting for her in her room later that evening.

"So what the hell was all that about?" Tanya asked. "You and the hydrant?"

"I was chatting with a water spirit who was passing through. Come to think of it, I should introduce you two next time she's in town. I'm sure you'd like her," Erin said, dropping a wink.

Tanya threw her hands up to the ceiling. She had promised herself she wouldn't do this, but there was no denying her frustration.

"I have to know. When we're not together, are you sleeping around with other…well, 'people', I guess."

"What's wrong?" Erin asked, frowning. "I thought you didn't want something serious. I thought you were looking for some fun."

"I'm not, and I do," Tanya answered, exasperated with her own ambivalence. She sighed. "I just want to make sure I'm not being used."

"You're not," Erin said. "This is fun for the both of us, isn't it?" She rose from the chair and approached Tanya slowly. "I get that you think I'm maybe not the most reliable of girlfriends. But let me make it up to you. If you want fun, I'll take you to the greatest party ever: the Conclave."

Tanya pricked up then. Erin had mentioned this place before. "Biggest bash in the two worlds," she had once said, "like Times Square on New Year's Eve all the time." She spoke about the Conclave with the same mix of anticipation and bravado that some of the boys at school who, unaware of her preferences-or worse yet, convinced they were 'virile' enough to overcome it-might say: "You've got to come to the Ceylon with me Friday night. It's the best bar in the city, and I know the bouncer so we don't have to worry about I.D."

In fact, Erin had said almost the exact same thing when Tanya had finally agreed to go to this Conclave. "Don't worry about not being a fairy. I've picked up a few tricks in my time and I'll whip up an aura for you that'll fool everybody into thinking you're a fey." That alone, Tanya now thought, should have been a warning to her. Passing for an adult and passing for an immortal were two rather different things.

It turned out that this Conclave wasn't just two buses and a metro away like the famed Ceylon Bar. It was in the Otherworld, the Fairy Realm. Asking for specifications on the nature of this plane was futile, however, as it appeared to defy comprehension for anybody who wasn't born into it.

The most pleasant way to access the Otherworld is to walk into mist, dissolve and be translated into the Undying Lands, but for Tanya and most other mortals, who possess an unfortunately fatal reaction to discorporation, another method was required. This involved tunnels deep in the earth that link one realm to another. Chasm City was apparently one of those places rich in such passageways. Tanya thought this rather convenient until Erin pointed out that she rarely ventured too far from such portals.

More logical in their presence but far more inconvenient were the sewers. Having informed Tanya's father that they would be staying over at Erin's house for a change, the pair set out with warm clothes and flashlights, walking with noses upturned into an open-air sewage pipe on the eastern side of the River Cherokee. Though the sewers initially had ramps on the side, as they went deeper the pipelines became narrower until they had to wade in the sludge.

"This is the most disgusting thing I've ever done," Tanya said.

"Well, don't look at me," Erin replied. "These tunnels used to be pristine, if a little damp. You breeders are the ones who decided this would be a cozy spot to plunk down a sewage system."

"*I* never made such a decision, and didn't I ask you to stop calling me a breeder?"

"Sorry. Hard to shake ancient habits. But you have to admit, the whole viviparous reproduction thing you guys have going on is pretty gross."

Tanya avoided a bit of unidentifiable flotsam only to step on something slimy at the bottom of the pipe and lose her footing. There was a surprised half-shout followed by an angry, repulsive gurgle.

Erin turned back to help Tanya out, getting covered in sewage as well. When both were standing again, Erin ran her hands over her body and was returned to an immaculate condition.

"I don't suppose you could use your amazing detergent powers on me?" Tanya asked, eyeing the spotless fairy before her with a small measure of resentment.

"Nope," Erin said with that joke-at-the-mortal's-expense smile. "Only fey need apply to the Erin Laundromat."

"You realize, of course, that I'm going to arrive at this great party of yours smelling like…well, the sewers."

"Don't worry about that. When we reach the Other Side, I'll be able to whip you up an ensemble as part of your fey fake I.D. It'll also eliminate any unseemly odors."

Tanya grunted something inaudible, but undoubtedly impolite, which just made Erin grin wider. "What happens we when come back the other way?" Tanya asked.

"Um…I guess you stink and walk around wearing sewage until we get back to your place and into your shower."

"You presume much, O enchanted one. I've not been having a good evening so far, and am not in a giving mood."

"You'll love the Conclave. You'll see."

The journey through the sewers lasted an hour and a half until they reached what seemed to be a standing wall of mist. Tanya hesitated before it, but Erin grabbed her arm and yanked her through. The tunnel on the other side looked like it was a natural formation of rock but was otherwise dark, musty and unremarkable. It took another fifteen minutes to reach the surface of this world, a pastoral landscape of rolling hills, wind-swept fields and clear blue skies.

True to her earlier promise, Erin wiggled her fingers and Tanya suddenly found the reek of the sewers gone and her dirty spring clothes replaced with a one-piece white gown which tied behind her neck but left her back bare. Erin herself had changed into a skin-tight pair of black leather trousers, with two thick straps judiciously crisscrossing her chest, attached to a neckband studded with small diamonds.

"Do you like it?" Erin asked, eyebrows doing an endearing wiggle.

Tanya took stock of her new garments. They could be generously described as billowy, and it felt as though she were wearing nothing. The wind picked up, and Tanya noted wryly that the cloth had a similar effect visually.

"Could I have something less diaphanous?"

"You're no fun," Erin said, but waved her hands again and Tanya watched her robe grow more opaque until there was something left to the imagination.

"So when do we get to this Conclave of yours?"

"Right now!"

Tanya watched in amazement as the world dissolved, fading like a snowy television reception, reforming into the inside of a great wooden hall with no ceiling, pillars arching above like branches with the depthless blue sky acting as the vaults. All around her beings of varying size and shape walked, caroused or lurched about, though the majority were human-looking, almost uniform in their stunning good looks. Their clothing had the same pseudoarchaic look that Erin had selected for them, the women wearing gowns of varied description, the males tending more towards togas and shirts with necklines so plunging they could more accurately be described as waistlines.

"We're always a couple of centuries behind the latest human fashion trends," Erin said with a shrug, as though reading her partner's mind. "I shudder to think what will happen when the Conclave discovers disco. C'mon, let's mingle."

Erin led them across the springy, earthen floor, weaving through couples and groups deep in conversation, dancing, drinking or fucking, past vaulted 'rooms' in the seemingly endless halls where fey folk sampled delicacies, listened to music played by disembodied instruments and voices, or lounged on the chaotically placed furniture. Five chambers in, a tall, lithe man with aristocratic features intercepted them.

"Hello Arawn," Erin said, none too pleased to see him.

"Greetings to you and your...companion," he said.

This particular specimen of *sidhe* wore a vivid red blouse and golden pantaloons, tied at the waist with a rawhide belt. "I'm afraid I don't know what name you are going by these days, Sheela Na Gig...?"

"Sheila who?" Tanya said.

"Erin, and never mind that. Tanya, this is Arawn of Annwn." Tanya noted that Erin had pronounced her name 'Ta-ni-a', perhaps thinking it sounded more apropos to their setting. "Arawn, this is Tanya Drake, a sylph most recently from America."

Arawn sniffed. "Graceless place." With an indolent glance at Erin, he leaned over to Tanya in a fluid motion until his mouth was by her ear. "A word of advice, girlfriend. Your new play-pal here is like a kelpie: she'll consume what she wants and then toss you aside."

He pulled out, favored Erin with a diligently insincere smile and brushed past them, disappearing into the teeming mass of fey folk.

"Kind of flaming, isn't he?" Tanya said.

"You have no idea," Erin replied, rolling her eyes. "That guy wouldn't touch a woman if she were lying in bed with him for a year. And I mean that literally."

"Say, what's a kelpie?"

"Uh…a cannibalistic phantom horse. With a Scottish accent. Why?"

"Never mind."

Erin eyed her suspiciously. "Never mind him," she said. "The party favors are up ahead."

The 'party favors' turned out to be an assortment of spices and herbs that could be chewed to produce diverse intoxicating effects.

"For a mortal like yourself, the hard stuff will either force your consciousness to expand until it reaches a higher plane of comprehension or it'll give you seizures," Erin explained. "It varies from person to person."

"…Yeah, I think I'll pass on the hard stuff; try something less risky."

"Good for you. Most people who achieve omniscience only wind up hating it anyway."

The 'soft' stuff itself was fairly intense to Tanya, who had never done anything harder than the occasional night of drinking and the odd French kiss with Mary Jane. Her senses felt heightened and precise, but at the same time she didn't feel light-headed or as though her thoughts were muddled, as she had with the mortal counterparts. With such receptivity, she gave herself fully over to the revelries of the night, the hours speeding away as she partook in the libertine lifestyle of the fairy folk. Erin had certainly spoken the truth: the Conclave was by far the best party she'd ever been to.

That was, until Erin suddenly stood up off the divan they were both lying on, causing Tanya to crash to the floor due to the fact that Erin had originally been underneath her.

"What the fuck?" Tanya demanded, rubbing her rump where she had taken the brunt of the impact.

"Shit. It's Oberon," Erin said, not really paying attention.

Tanya followed her lover's gaze to a tall, stately-looking man with snowy white hair hanging past his shoulders. He was dressed in a folded white robe shot through with treads of gold, tied at the waist with a turquoise sash. He was surrounded by a coterie of other fairies as he walked, like a faintly absurd posse of male supermodels. Even from this distance (though perhaps aided by the drugs) she could see the light grey irises of his eyes, but mortal senses alone were sufficient to pick up the intense power that radiated from him.

Tanya felt a hand on the collar of her dress and was suddenly yanked backwards, up and over the divan, landing on the other side with a thud and probably bruising the other cheek in the process. Erin was beside her, having apparently been the one doing the yanking.

"What's the big idea?"

Erin didn't answer. She glanced over the top of the divan, and then lowered herself again, coming to rest with her back against the upholstery. Tanya slid alongside her, feeling vaguely like a pair of misbehaving children hiding behind the couch from their parents. Erin wasn't smiling, which was rather unusual for her.

"When you say 'Oberon'…is that the same Oberon from the play?"

"Yeah, that's him. Or as close an approximation as a Renaissance playwright can get, anyway. Though you'd be well advised not to mention that particular story around here. Oberon is the oldest fairy, and as such the *de facto* leader around here. He's got this terribly annoying delusion of dignity, and absolutely hates being made fun of."

Erin glanced around before continuing, as though making sure nobody was listening in—an act which Tanya found somewhat ridiculous, given how deeply the fey around them were wrapped up in their own hedonistic pursuits.

"So you can imagine how absolutely thrilled he was when he found out that what was originally gossip for the Otherworld was now all over England—and eventually all over the world—because this one fairy decided to share this tittle-tattle with his mortal lover, who goes on to make dunces of the king and queen of fairyland in iambic pentameter."

"His lover? Wait, Shakespeare was gay?"

"Bi. Hello? Have you not *read* the sonnets? When he goes about how he's torn between two lovers, a dark lady and a younger man?" Erin seemed to grow distant. "Of course, the fey in question was probably older than Shakespeare by an exponential factor. Aren't they supposed to teach you this stuff in school?"

"Catholic school, remember? Gay people are about as real to them as…well, you lot to the rest of the world."

"Anyway," Erin went on, "Oberon was furious. This is a guy who has a stick up his ass the size of a baobab under normal circumstances, and the last millennium has been particularly bad because of those very same marriage troubles that your Shakespeare popularized. And all this because Titania had her sights set on some newly coalesced fey—a changeling—and the Big O wanted to get a piece of that ass first. Well, Titania gets into a huff and says 'Fine, you can have him—but you won't have me', and she's refused to have sex with him ever since."

"So basically, Oberon is pissed off because he's not getting any," Tanya concluded.

"That pretty much sums it up, yeah."

"I don't get it. If they were both going to bang this changeling, then couldn't he just go outside of his marriage for sex?"

"Oh, sure. Monogamy doesn't exist here. Honestly, it truly takes somebody who only lives for seventy-odd years to conceive of making lifetime commitments to another, single person. I don't care how much two people claim to love each other; spend a few centuries together and I'll bet they'll be desperate for other prospects. But Titania..." Erin drifted off wistfully. "The older you are, the more tricks you build up, so just try to imagine what she knows...things that could drive mortals insane. For Oberon to be denied this after being together since time immemorial...I imagine it's rather like withdrawal."

"You guys sure do like your sex tricks," Tanya said.

"Well, when you can live forever without having to worry about things like paying the rent, pretty much the only thing you want to do is have fun. And when you get to be as old as we do, there's a premium on originality and diversity of experience. There's a reason why mortals who stumble into here, afterwards, often think they've entered some kind of heavenly afterlife, you know."

Erin poked her head around the divan, blowing air from her lips in frustration when she pulled back again.

"Damn it, he's still there. He just *had* to pick that spot for a conversation."

"So we're avoiding this guy because he's a prig?"

"Well, there's the prig thing, and there's also the fact that after the incident with the play, Oberon sort of declared an interdiction on relationships between fairies and mortals."

"Say what?" Tanya whispered harshly.

Erin winced. "Yeah. I suppose he figured that he couldn't do anything about us gossiping, but he could prevent the mortal world from making a further mockery of him by forbidding the kind of trysts that led to your people getting wind of all this in the first place."

"Bleeding hell, why didn't you say anything about this sooner?"

"What for?" Erin asked, annoyed.

"What for?" Tanya repeated. "How could you bring me here when you knew our relationship is taboo in your world?"

"Our relationship isn't exactly well-looked on in your world either, you know," Erin riposted.

"Yeah, but the bigoted old men of my world don't have supernatural powers." Realizing she was practically hissing, Tanya closed her eyes and focused on breathing, trying to calm down. "What about my fairy cloaking field? I thought you said it would let me pass for a fey?"

"It does. The problem is Oberon walks around with a complete Otherworldly population database behind those grey eyes of his. If he saw you, he'd know you were a mortal because he wouldn't recognize you."

"Okay, that's bad. What happens if we're found out?"

"For me, Oberon's little band of cronies takes away my abilities to transfer between the worlds for a period of time—usually a century or two. For you…the memory of your time here in Otherworld."

"And that's worse," Tanya said, running a hand through her short-cropped hair. "Jesus Q*bert Christ, how can you do this to me?"

"It's not *that* big a deal," Erin said, looking set-upon. "I can see some distinctive advantages to a memory wipe. You'll get to experience everything you've forgotten as if it were the first time. I know *I'd* love to see that stunned expression on your face the first time I turned translucent in front of you once more."

Tanya seized the fairy's shoulder. "Maybe getting your memory erased sounds like a jolly good time to *you*, but *I'm not you*. I don't live for millennia, I haven't had sex with an assortment of historical figures, and I can't control my body at the subatomic level. Being mortal means that you have to balance any desire to seek out new experiences with the fact that you could easily *die*, and then you wouldn't experience anything *at all*! Like you insist on pointing out at every opportunity, we only live for a set amount of time, and losing some memory is like getting our lifespan shortened even more."

Erin's face had set into an impassive façade. "You see, this sort of melodrama is exactly the reason why most fairies don't even try dating you breeders."

Tanya crossed her arms over her chest and looked at Erin levelly. The *sidhe* woman had the good sense to wince, perhaps realizing she had crossed a line. "Look, baby, I didn't mean it that way. Honestly, it came out wrong."

But Tanya was unyielding. "When your buddy Oberon finally buggers off, I want you to take me home."

"Tanya, I'm sorry, okay? I realize now that I should have told you earlier. But you don't really want to leave a party like this."

"You'll take me home," Tanya repeated.

"You'll change your mind," Erin said, but mostly to herself.

Tanya and Erin spent several more minutes of relative time behind the couch, neither talking nor looking at each other. Occasionally, Erin would poke her head around the side or above the upholstery, checking on Oberon's progress. Tanya, biting her lip, was trying to think of a way to lighten the tension when the couch they were hiding behind suddenly pushed up against them.

"Hey, menhir-butt!" Erin called out, pushing herself up onto all fours. "Be careful where you park that thing!"

Tanya looked up and was surprised to recognize the fey that faced them. Arawn of Annwn's face went from indignation to indignation mixed with perplexity as he recognized them in turn.

"What are you two doing down there?"

"We're examining the wood grain," Erin said before Tanya could say anything.

Arawn blinked at her. "We don't have wooden floors."

"We're using the power of imagination."

Arawn frowned, looking at her, and then glanced about. When he turned back to them, a sly smile split his aristocratic features. "You wouldn't be back there because it's out of the Great Grump's line of sight, would you?"

"Of course not. Now do you mind? We intend to imagine some marble tiles next, and we need to concentrate."

"My apologies," Arawn said in that particularly insincere way of his, and Tanya tensed, certain something bad was going to follow. Arawn rose from the divan, stepped to the side, and appeared to walk away when he flipped one leg backwards, catching the couch beneath an armrest. Despite his lithe figure, the divan went airborne before crashing back down with a loud splintery sound. Tanya, surprised, stood up suddenly, her arms before her as though to ward off bits of divan debris.

Arawn put a hand to the side of his lips. "Oops."

As the sound of the crashed couch resonated in the high-vaulted hall, Tanya saw the heads of nearby fey snap in their direction—including the white-garbed statesman at the center of the supermodel posse. Despite the distance separating them,

Tanya felt his grey eyes lock onto hers, saw something bright and harsh flash there. Tanya wondered if this was how bacterial cultures felt when examined through microscopes.

She blinked to dispel the unpleasant sensation of being visually dissected, but in the split-second of darkness Oberon somehow teleported himself forward. He now stood right before her. Tanya let out a gasp and took a step backwards, but could go no further. Oberon's grey eyes, zigzagged with bolts of spiteful lightning, had transfixed her somehow, and she was helpless to do anything but tilt her head back as he lifted his graceful hand to her chin.

"What have we here?" he asked, his voice smooth, melodious and laced with menace. "I don't recognize you, and you're far too old to have just coalesced. Has a nasty little breeder stumbled into Our Kingdom?"

"My liege," Erin said, scrambling to her feet. "My lord, my king…I can explain. It's not what you think."

Oberon favored Erin with a cruelly magnanimous smile. "You know this woman, my child? Then surely you can account for her presence here."

He extended his hand towards her, as though granting permission for her to start. Tanya, stiff beneath whatever trance Oberon had cast over her, watched out of the corner of her eyes as Erin licked her lips. Oberon waited with a predator's patience.

"I had this one fetch the mortal for me."

If Erin's voice was melodious, the woman who now stood behind her had the full metropolitan orchestra playing her vocal cords. She stepped into Tanya's peripheral vision, and had Tanya not been fixed in place, she would have been rocked back by the woman's grace and beauty. If a Platonic ideal lurked behind every painting of the female form in the last five hundred years, this was surely it.

"My queen!" Erin said, happy and relieved. Because it

seemed appropriate, Tanya echoed Erin's words, although since she was gripped by Oberon's will, it came out more like "I keen!"…which, at the moment, was not untrue either.

Oberon did not seem pleased to see his wife. His smile went from predatory to outright feral. "Did you really, my love?" he asked pleasantly through gritted teeth. "Surely one as wise as yourself would know better than to defy my edicts."

Titania laughed, a tinkling of chimes. "You believe I am sleeping with this drudge? Your opinion of me has indeed fallen to abyssal depths, husband, if you think I would lower myself to such bestiality."

Tanya was about to object (mush-mouthed though she was), but caught herself in time. For whatever reason, Titania was actually helping her, and it was best to play along. And Tanya was honest enough to admit that Titania was stratospheres out of her league. Still…she had to admit that it stung.

"Nonsense—I have always thought most highly of you, my queen," Oberon said with edged courtesy. "Yet I cannot help but continue to wonder at this breeder's presence here. Perhaps you would care to enlighten us?"

"I trust my lord has not forgotten mortals have uses other than sex. I have brought her here to serve as my handmaiden."

"Is that so?" Oberon turned his attention back to Tanya, and she felt whatever force that transfixed her let up, releasing her. Her relief was short-lived, however, as Oberon raised a slender finger and then asked Tanya: "And tell me, helpful little breeder, in what manner are you assisting my wife?"

Tanya glanced at Erin, who was chewing her bottom lip, and at Titania, who was waiting expectantly. She was not alone: a coliseum's worth of fey folk had gathered around them, watching the confrontation unfold with greedy, wanton stares. Tanya realized that nobody was going to jump in to answer the Big O this time. But what could she possibly have to offer as aide to entities that seemingly had such total control of themselves and their environments?

"Fashion," Tanya said.

"I beg your pardon?" Oberon said, his smile falling. His face actually looked less menacing without it.

"Fashion," Tanya repeated. "Isn't it obvious? You people are wearing styles that are so tragically passé that you need sundials to express just how dated they are. My lady recruited me to help her update her image to something a little less archaic. After all, it is only right that the queen of all fairies be the first in all fashions, the trendsetter."

Titania smiled beatifically at Oberon. "Surely you would not begrudge me my little passions?"

Tanya could tell from the thunderclouds brewing in his eyes that Oberon didn't believe a word of it, but the smile crept back onto his face and he parted his hands with a little bow.

"Nothing but the best for my queen, of course. I trust you will remember to wipe the revolting thing's memory before you return her to whatever cesspool you dredged her from?"

"But of course."

Oberon made a little bow again, pearly white teeth clenched so tight Tanya was amazed they didn't snap from the pressure. Then he spun around brusquely, stalking away, indicating with a sharp motion of his hand for his supermodel posse to follow him. Gradually, the other fairies dispersed. As Titania turned to leave (she had her own posse, Tanya noted, all female in opposition to her husband's clique), Tanya reached out to her.

"Wait! Thank you. I really appreciate the save."

Titania looked at Tanya's extended hand as one might observe a shaggy, greenish substance found at the back of the refrigerator.

"Child, I strongly suggest you remove yourself from this place before that great boor changes his mind and decides to rearrange the order of your vertebrae."

Titania turned and walked away, smoothly vanishing into

the center of her fairy escort.

Erin breathed a loud sigh of relief, and Tanya jumped, having almost forgotten about her nominal girlfriend.

"That was too close," she said.

"I don't understand," Tanya said. "She helped us…"

"Incidentally, maybe," Erin said. "Mostly, she just wanted to spite the Big O. Titania is eternal royalty—she would never condescend to consort with me, let alone you."

Tanya had quite enough of being insulted for one night. She turned as flinty a stare as she could manage (inspiring herself from Oberon's) onto Erin, and the fey woman had the decency to look contrite.

"Well, you heard the lady. Get me out of here."

Erin opened her mouth as though to protest, saw Tanya's expression, and seemed to think better of it. She nodded and guided Tanya to a part of the great wooden hall more adapted to transduction across the Otherworld. In a moment, Erin returned them to the mouth of the cavern they had used to gain access to these Undying Lands. They trudged in silence through the caves, and when they reached the veil that separated the two realities from one another, Tanya walked through first with no need of encouragement from Erin. They wallowed through the sewers on the other side, back in their mortal clothes, the frosty hush between them even heavier than the scent of rot and decay in the pipelines. Erin accompanied Tanya to the mouth of the open grate on the banks of the Cherokee.

"So this is it," Erin said when Tanya stopped to look back.

"Pretty much, yes. As dumping grounds go, I'd say it's fairly appropriate."

"Look, for what it's worth, I am sorry. The Conclave is so huge that I thought we could spend years there and never bump into Oberon. It was just bad luck."

"What about the other fairies?"

"Oh, they wouldn't have said anything even if they had

found out. By law we aren't supposed to have relationships with humans, but a lot of fey folk come here on the down low for a bit of snooker every once and a while. We just don't talk about it."

"Don't ask, don't tell," Tanya said wryly.

"I've never really looked at it that way...but yes, I suppose that's true."

Tanya shook her head. "It's not just about tonight, Erin—though I'm really pissed, make no mistake about that. You're always trying to put yourself in a position of superiority over me, sharing just enough so I can be awed by you. Well, the effect has worn off. You've never respected me as a person—as a *mortal* person—and I'm tired of being your groupie. I'm just entertainment to you, a break from fucking other fairies in your Conclave. It was fun while it lasted, but I'm moving on. My life is short."

"You know, I never took you for the type to walk away from something because somebody else forbade it. You're just letting them win."

"I'm not that type, and you damned well know it. I'm also not the type to let myself be treated shoddily. I'm not letting anybody win; I'm making sure I don't lose."

"It was fun though, wasn't it?" Erin said after several moments' silence, with one last attempt at an ingratiating smile.

"Goodbye, Erin," Tanya said, not unkindly.

"Goodbye, Tanya," Erin said, somewhat crestfallen. "Take care of yourself, kid." With that she turned around and vanished into the tunnel, seeming to dissolve into the darkness. Tanya turned around, facing the city again, and made her way back home. She slipped into the apartment she shared with her father, trying not to wake him, and took a very long shower, alone, trying to get the stink of the sewers off. She had the impression that it might be a few days yet before she would feel entirely clean, and it wasn't just the sewage.

In the months since that break-up, Tanya's thoughts would often turn back to Erin. She would remember the way she would smile, or laugh, or toss back that great mane of red hair. She would recall the night they went to the Conclave, the ridiculous dress she wore and Erin's leathery outfit; bring to mind the chaotic saturnalia within the wooden halls and the mind-bending herbs. She would remember her fury at discovering the peril she'd been callously placed into, squirming (figuratively) beneath Oberon's thunderous grey gaze, and the atypically cheerless shape of Erin as she disappeared from her life. She would wonder, occasionally, whether she would be able to find her way back to the misty curtain separating the worlds from another by herself, or whether Erin was down there even now, introducing another girl to the pleasures of the Otherworld.

But mostly she remembered the pillow-talk. Lying in bed, feeling relaxed and at ease, until hearing from next to her: "Some of the kinkiest sex I've ever had was in Egypt, about two thousand years ago. You'd be amazed the things Cleopatra could do with only her nose."

Under Suspicion

Dr. Philip Edward Kaldon

That first moment, when the warning alarms sounded, Ensign Lily Branoch's blood ran cold. Like everyone else who worked in space Lily maintained constant awareness of the nearest airlock, spacesuit, fire suppresser, medkit and the distance to the nearest hardened bulkhead—six meters—before the overhead shipwide speakers clicked for the announcement. "ALL HANDS, ALL HANDS. MEDICAL EMERGENCY IN THE MAIN HANGAR—HEAVY ACCIDENT. RESCUE CREWS REPORT IMMEDIATELY. NO FIRE, NO TOXIC, NO VACUUM. CLEAR CORRIDORS FORWARD OF MAIN HANGAR FOR TRAUMA TEAMS. THIS IS NOT A DRILL. TIME MARK—FIFTEEN SECONDS."

Relief she wasn't in personal danger was swiftly followed by action. Lily sprinted towards the bulkhead, concerned an industrial accident in the main hangar could involve her people. She stripped off her uniform jacket along the way and in her short-sleeved white shirt backed into an emergency medpack, pulled the padded straps over her arms and latched the waist cinch.

As Lily arrived on the scene, the overhead speakers announced a time mark of forty-five seconds since the accident and all of the overhead lights blazed full on. Inside the hangar, cargotainers were stacked three and four meters high, except where one pile had toppled. A walking loader frame, which boosted the reach of a deckhand, lay on its side nearby. Lily could see the legs of at least three crewman under the unstable pile. She wore only standard safety gear, including a hard helmet, plus the medpack, so she ran to the man inside the loader frame. A Marine in heavy powered armor already moved to assist the trapped crewmen.

"Spaceman Heiden," Lily read the name tag on the man's jumpsuit. A lock of blond hair fell in her face—she automatically brushed it back, pinning it behind an ear. "Can you hear me?"

He made no immediate response. Lily folded down the arms of her medpack and spread out the array of trays. She ran her hands through the ring of a filmer, and once they were encased, slipped on a diagnostic palm link and held her left hand to the man's wrist, then his neck. Blood pooled slowly under the man's head.

"One minute thirty," a voice said in her earpiece. "Medcheck, Mister Branoch."

"Spaceman Heiden, male, twentyish, bleeding from head, pulse and respiration datalinked—they're acceptable—unconscious. Located inside the downed loader frame."

"Roger, sir. Other injuries?"

"I just got here, Medcheck," Lily said.

"Understood, sir. Take it easy—we have time."

The whine of hydraulic assists and the clatter of rubberized metal on metal told Lily the cargotainers were being moved. She tried not to watch them, hoped that the remaining pile wouldn't slip her way.

"Careful there!" a new voice shouted. "We've got people under here!"

"Aye-aye, lieutenant—careful is our central operating procedure."

"See that it is—carry on."

Lily glanced up to see a woman crouched down on the other side of the loader frame. At first the impression was all long dark shiny black hair and well-tanned arms, then the woman turned towards Lily. From her white T-shirt and scarlet running shorts the newcomer had to be a Marine.

"Let me use your filmer," the Marine said quietly. "I've got a man down under this frame."

Automatically Lily held out her left arm over the tubes and beams of the loader, letting the filmer ring pop out.

"Are any of these men yours?" the Marine asked.

"Uh...no," Lily said. "I don't think so. This looks like a food stores load—not my area."

"That's good."

"Any yours?"

The Marine gave a brief nod over her shoulder. "First Sergeant Dupris was working the check-in podium. A container hit the deck and bounced off his leg."

"He's lucky."

"Yeah, Doc can squirt in some bone glue and Dupris will be back on duty tomorrow," the Marine said. "Can we move this frame? This man's leg is pinned."

"I've got the loader shut down and safed," Lily said. "How much clearance do you need to pull him out?"

"The boot is caught—a centimeter or two will do it."

"There's a jack in the back of this pack."

"Got it," the Marine said, sprinting around to get the small bright yellow wedge. The waistband of her running shorts held one of the ubiquitous tiny ultra-compressed air cylinders. It'd be enough for three minutes of breathing or, in this case, provide enough pressure to raise the jack.

"Lift point is that block right where those two pieces meet," Lily pointed. "You got it."

The loader frame shifted just slightly, not enough to even move its operator, but sufficient to shift the boot free. In the minute Lily spent working to free Heiden's safety straps from the loader frame, the Marine had worked on her injured man and they were already gone. Lily couldn't have told anyone the hair color of the crewman lying in front of her—but she could detail the color of this woman's eyes, describe the shape and curl of her long dark eyelashes, the light flare of her nostrils as she breathed and that she wasn't wearing a bra under her sweaty white T-shirt.

Spaceman Heiden was swiftly transferred to a gurney loaded with diagnostic computers while a vampire pack was fitted to his arm. The temporary spray-on bandage Lily had applied to the head wound looked like it would hold long enough to get him to Sick Bay.

"Hey aren't you the Junior Cargo Officer?"

Lily looked up to see one of the mid-level engineering officers. The *Mastodon* was a large enough ship that not all the ensigns were known shipwide. "Yessir," she said after getting up and saluting. "Ensign Lily Branoch, sir."

"You qualified to pull this unit's black cards?"

"Absolutely."

"Then sign on this unit and take possession of both black cards for the accident investigation."

"There are three black cards on this unit, sir."

The lieutenant was taken aback for a moment. "You know these damned things better than I do then. Pull all the cards and get a stop gap card inserted ASAP."

"Yes, sir."

Though the loader frame's computers were datalinked to the ship, monitoring data was also backed up on the series of so-called black cards, which Lily removed. Getting an evidence envelope from the bosun's mate, she sealed the black cards inside. That done, there was really nothing left for her to do, but she went around and offered help anyway.

One of the fallen cargotainers had split open, leaving cans scattered across the deck, some leaking; Lily caught the sweet scent of peaches in the air.

◆◆◆

Once all the injured had been moved to Sick Bay, the hangar was locked down. Clean up would wait until the more senior officers came down and did an inspection. Senior Chief Felipe Armande, a short, wiry Canadian, headed up Lily's main cargo handling team. He came over with a cup of coffee to where she sat leaning against the empty loader frame lying on the deck.

"Here you go, sir. You look like you need this more than I do."

"Thanks, chief," Lily said, grateful for the strong Navy coffee.

"Rough morning," he said, observing the chaos around them. "Bad day for everyone."

"I suppose we're going to be on the investigation team," she said.

"That's what I hear—since it wasn't our people involved."

"Have you seen the viddie from the security cams yet?"

"Yeah, looks like a malfunction. Heiden shifted that cargotainer from the station sled to Alpha stack, then he stopped, wobbled twice and crashed into the stack. Looked like he was having a helluva time trying to keep it upright."

"Sounds like equipment failure and not operator error."

"Yessir. Control unit? Balance sensor? Hydraulics? Don't know yet. Anything else, sir?"

She wanted to ask, *Yes, who was that beautiful woman I saw today?* "No, chief. Thanks for the coffee."

"You're most welcome, sir. Better go and get cleaned up before the brass come down."

◆◆◆

The investigation team met briefly at 0800 hours the next morning and exchanged data files. Though unlikely, there could be a more formal board of inquiry convened the next time they were in a Fleet administrative port.

"Ensign Branoch—have you examined the black cards from this loader frame?"

This would be her one real contribution to the report.

"Yes, sir. At 0830 hours 27 seconds, a sensor noted a pressure drop on Primary Hydraulic Circuit 3. The system attempted to compensate, but the pump had seized. Spaceman Heiden was in the middle of a stacking maneuver. There was insufficient hydraulic pressure to regain control of the unit before it fell into Alpha stack."

"Doesn't this unit have redundant hydraulic capacity?"

"Yes, sir. There was also a malfunctioning mixer valve between Hydraulic Circuits 2 and 3. It failed to open under the pressure loss. Equipment failure—entropy, sir."

The next question was a surprise. "Ensign, is this model loader frame designed to stack cargotainers to the height utilized in this operation?"

"Yes, sir."

"But you wouldn't recommend it for your own crew."

"Sir, my cargo handling unit does not move food stores. Often our cargotainers are much larger and heavier than these. So no, I don't recommend a maneuver like this for my operations."

"Thank you, ensign."

Lily got the distinct impression that the senior officer had been hoping for a different answer.

The questions turned to the emergency and medical response times, effectiveness ratings. Lily's attention wandered to the data board in front of her. Skimming through the preliminary report, she found an appendix that listed every person who'd participated. Seventeen Marines were listed, but unfortunately, all names were given in military form—rank, first initial, last name—and she hardly knew any of the Marines serving aboard the *Mastodon*.

As an officer, Lily had the authority to call up personnel records including photos. But she didn't have a good reason to do so. And one very good reason *not to*—it was an unconscionable breech of protocol to do so for personal reasons. Besides, Marines were redeployed all the time. How long could such a relationship last? And that was assuming this Marine liked girls at all. The odds were against her. So Lily restrained herself.

◆◆◆

The medium attack cruiser *Mastodon* (CFG-441) was one of some 25,000 ships in the Unified Star Fleet trying to keep the peace and regulate the diaspora of humanity throughout half a billion cubic light years of space in the West Orion Arm of the galaxy. Today they were on their third day in port at Chalet Station, high above Aurica IV. This was a first-class operation for supplies, which made Lily's work easier, and Fleet liked the place because it boasted a heavy repair facility for large starliners, which could also accommodate midsize warships. The *Mastodon* had entered service in 2679 and was finishing its second century of operations. Unlike the water navies of Earth, starships didn't corrode and wear out so rapidly in the vacuum of deep space and two hundred years was probably close to average age of the Fleet. But they still needed to keep up on the maintenance.

The ship's Cargo Control was located just off the main hangar. Thick quad-glazed plex windows, plus the meter-and-a-half raised floor, allowed a good view of operations in isolated safety. Often this command and office space was empty—Lily frequently used it as a convenient place to catch up on paperwork, hiding in plain sight. Being in port meant they were blessed with regular communications from Earth. So that's why Lily was in Cargo Control at the start of this shift—reading the latest messages from her mother in Minneapolis.

You'll always be a special girl, sweetheart.

Lily sighed. Her mother was always writing such things, meant to be inspirational, but what they really accomplished was transmitting the disappointment in choosing an off-world military career over the more expected threesome of

Minnesota, marriage and motherhood. Lily's mother still saw the awkward ditzy blond tomboy of nine, not the successful commissioned officer in the Unified Star Fleet. So much for her excellent grades, numerous commendations earned at the Academy and her spotless service record. Worse were her mother's suggestions that "playing in the military" would hurt Lily's chances of landing a suitable husband. *Mom!* Lily wanted to shout across the hundreds of light years of space. *I'm gay! Remember?*

"Good news? Bad news?"

Lily looked up to see Senior Chief Armande standing not two meters from where she sat. "Ah...no, chief."

"Neither one? That's a pretty good trick, sir."

"Um, it's my mother."

"Again."

"Yeah. She sends me notes—she means well, but..."

"Ah, you don't have to say anything more. Many a child has been driven to drink by a well-meaning mother."

"Then you do understand," inwardly wincing at the thought she'd just suggested to the NCO she supervised that her mother was driving her to drink.

"Not at all," Armande laughed. "My mother is a saint and her children all revere her." Lily must've appeared crestfallen, because he hastily added, "I'm just kidding, sir. Can I buy you a drink later to make up for it?"

"Sorry, chief. I have fire watch tonight."

"Oh well," the chief said. "Another time maybe."

"Sure."

Lily sighed after he'd left, relieved to be alone again. *I'm making a black hole out of nothing. This is just my mother driving me crazy.* She pocketed her datapad—time to get herself squared away and start her rounds, the first of the day.

Aboard the Unified Star Fleet medium attack cruiser Mastodon, Ensign Lily Branoch was the moral equivalent of a glorified file clerk. Or at least that's what she felt most days. Technically her title was Junior Cargo Officer and her responsibilities covered a wide range of areas. She was in charge of anything from weapons to uniforms to electronics to hotel services—everything but food—that could be stowed in a cargo bay.

Besides checking things in and making sure requisition requests were being funneled to the appropriate procurement officers, Lily also had to walk the hangar and cargo decks of the *Mastodon*. She'd just entered Cargo Bay 6 when a mechanical commotion from behind attracted her attention.

A five-man squad of fully suited armored Marines entered. Lily loved to watch these oversized black spacesuits move with their powered assist—such a complex ballet of operator and machine. A good marine could pick up an egg with an armored gauntlet and not crush it. An exceptional marine could bathe a baby and change its diaper without causing injury.

One of the five hulking suits stopped in front of Lily and saluted. The machine sighed as its environmental backpack opened a vent and began to exchange air between suit and cargo bay. Stenciled letters on the reveal strip of the suit's chest pack read 2ND LT. CRUZ-ORTEGA. The helmet remained closed and dark as the speaker on the chest pack came live.

"Sir," Cruz-Ortega said in a voice electronically stripped of any identifying tonal color. "Request permission to secure this cargo bay as a forward changing zone. My men and I would like to break out of this armor, but we're on a Ready Five status for immediate re-deploy."

"Of course, Lieutenant." Lily touched her databoard and made the assignment. Fostering good relations with the Marine detachment that provided their security was a call she could make without getting it confirmed by her boss, Lt. Commander Saxon, or a command officer. "If you'd sign?"

She expected the Marine officer to transmit an electronic

confirmation, but instead this one took the databoard and stylus, scribbled a legible signature and handed it back, turned and signaled to the other marines.

"Squad Eight! Break out and stand down."

A chorus of acknowledgments answered the lieutenant. While the cargo bay didn't have changing frames for the armor suits, they were able to lock onto the utility rail running along the bulkhead to keep the suits from falling over. As five helmets came off, chest packs swung round allowing the fronts of the suits to fold open. Lily hung around to watch, curious to see their faces.

Lt. Cruz-Ortega was *the* woman from the hangar deck. All cleaned up and in working uniform—mottled gray space camouflage pants and black tank top—she was gorgeous. Near to Lily's own height, but without the deficiency of her pale blonde complexion. Long shiny black hair tightly knotted and tied out of the way. And though not obscenely ripped, Cruz-Ortega's arm muscles were well-defined and she moved with a grace indicating complete control of her body.

Lily couldn't stop staring. And when the lieutenant looked over at Lily, she smiled and winked before turning away and tending to her machinery. Then Lily realized that the rest of the marines were watching her ogle Cruz-Ortega—she made a hasty retreat from the cargo bay. The marines never saw her blush.

◆◆◆

In college Lily once dated a sorority girl. Why it lasted nearly two years she could no longer fathom—perhaps it'd just been too comfortable to leave. Today she chalked it up to a learning experience. A Southern girl, Jasmine had tried to change Lily. So she dressed up better, had her hair colored and processed, and ate vegetarian—everything she wasn't.

The day they broke up, Lily 'celebrated' her independence with an enormous cheeseburger. It might've totally upset her digestion, this sudden onslaught of meat, except she'd been cheating with frequent cheeseburgers anyway, so perhaps she'd known the relationship was over for a long time. It annoyed Lily to have thoughts of her previous failed relationships rise to the surface as she made her afternoon rounds.

Cargo Bay 12 was the smallest in the ship, but it could still stack 625 meter-long weapons pallets. A long line of bots rolled in with fresh supplies. Two of Lily's crewmen worked the open-framed loaders, very similar operationally to the Marine's armor. Loaders provided hydraulic boost so one person could lift far beyond their capability and place the pallets higher than they could reach.

The cargo bay was also directly adjacent to the Marine barracks. Their armored airlock doors were opened, too, and she could see Marines exercising, training and lifting weights inside. As she scanned the bar codes on each pallet and checked them off her databoard, Lily periodically looked through the open doors on the far side of the bay to scan the Marine barracks for Cruz-Ortega.

Suddenly she spotted her quarry in black running shorts and a bright scarlet USFMC singlet. Hair tied back in a loose ponytail, her well-tanned skin, glistening with a film of light sweat from exertion, Cruz-Ortega jumped up half a meter, grabbed an overhead sissy bar and began doing rapid chin-ups.

Be still my beating heart...

"Ensign Branoch?"

Lily tried not to be too startled as her daydreaming was interrupted. "Yes?"

The officer standing there wasn't one she recognized. Indeed, his uniform bore an insignia for the Fleet supply ship *Overton*, not the *Mastodon*. He held out a databoard. "Is this your signature?"

"Who are you, lieutenant?" she asked, taking the databoard.

"Leland Walsh."

"Mister Walsh, this is a restricted cargo bay. How did you get in here?"

"These are my weapons you're loading. They're not quite signed for."

Still puzzled, Lily looked at the databoard. "This signature is from the Senior Cargo Officer, Lt. Commander Saxon. I don't know what the mystery is—his ID code is embedded in your document."

"Yes. Well, my petty officer was interrupted—only the first page is signed. I need a valid signature on each of these eight pages before you can keep these weapons."

Lily glanced at the other pages. Sure enough, the remaining signature fields were all blank. She took the stylus and signed.

"You helped out with the accident response in the hangar the other day, didn't you?" Walsh asked.

"Yes," she said, irritated that she still wasn't in control of this conversation. "You were there?"

"Oh sure. I was coming from a meeting with the third officer about your weapons order when the loader fell over. One helluva mess. Anyway, I thought I saw you there. You had the presence of mind to come in with a medpack. Good call."

"Thanks. Now. . ."

"Say, wasn't she there, too?"

Lily followed his gaze and realized he was admiring Cruz-Ortega's chin-ups over in the Marine barracks. "Uh, yeah," she said, handing back the databoard.

"Okay—I'm on my way. Thanks for the paperwork—the weapons are yours."

A waiting bot's angry warning blast broke Lily from her own sightseeing. She quickly scanned the pallets and sent the bot on its way. No one else seemed to notice her moment of distraction. When she looked back, the Marine lieutenant was no longer in view.

◆◆◆

Being an officer, it was relatively easy for Lily to go ashore for a drink. So, once off-duty, she headed immediately to the Relatively Harmless Bar. She'd had the intention of trying their signature single malt, but once there, filled with misery over her sudden crush, she decided instead to nurse a brandy old-fashioned, heavy on the fruit.

As she drank, Lily sifted through her dating strategies. Did she know any Marines who could introduce them? None came to mind—Lt. Cruz-Ortega's unit had just joined the ship. How could she know that the lieutenant was even interested? Sure, she'd smiled and winked at Lily, a common enough reaction from a Marine to a young blonde, but that didn't mean she was a lesbian.

She hated this constant second-guessing.

Lily went to take another sip of her drink only to have the straw suck up nothing but fumes. Fishing out the little spear with three maraschino cherries—or what were purported to be maraschino cherries on this space station, who could tell—and an orange slice, she held out the empty glass.

"I'll take another," she said. "Make it a double."

◆◆◆

Cargo Bays 8 and 10 both lay open and connected at this late hour. Lily knew they'd be filled in the morning with cargotainers bound to a contractor operating near The Fringe—dicey territory, hence FLEETCOM's sending a cruiser to do freighter work. Now they were empty space, save for two waiting loader frames and...

She stopped by the hatch frame and stared. In the dim of the overnight lighting, Lt. Cruz-Ortega was using the open space to run through a martial arts routine. It was beautiful, fast...*precise*.

Halfway through a complex motion, drawing in a deep clearing breath through pursed lips, the Marine officer spotted Lily and smoothly ended her routine. "I usually charge admission to watch a performance," Cruz-Ortega said.

"And I usually charge a studio rental fee for using my cargo bays."

Cruz-Ortega nodded. "Truce?"

"Truce."

"Good. Because I needed an excuse to take a break." More relaxed now, Cruz-Ortega walked over to where she'd left a towel and a water bottle. "We've never been properly introduced—Daniella Cruz-Ortega."

"Lily Branoch."

They shook hands.

"So is this training or recreation?" Lily asked.

"Possibly a little bit of both," Daniella said. "I'm not old—twenty-five—but I've got eighteen- and nineteen-year-olds working for me. They just live for finding a way to make the lieutenant look bad."

"Twenty-five's not old."

"Thank you."

"Though it's a year older than me," Lily said with a smirk.

"Touché." Daniella finished her water, then nodded at one of the frames. "Do you know how to run these loaders?"

"Sure—I have to prove myself to my eighteen-year-old Basic Spacemen, too."

"Can you show me?"

"I don't know how different it is from the armor you wear."

"I imagine it's a lot the same." Daniella slipped between the girder and padded tubing of a loader frame and settled in. Wiggling her hips, she found the directional pressure pads. "Very similar, I think."

"Despite the accident the other day," Lily said, "the loaders are really quite safe."

"I never thought otherwise," Daniella said. "Your testimony convinced me that it truly was an accident. I never expect lightning to strike twice in the same place—even harder inside a starship."

"What are you up to?" Lily asked, climbing into the other unit. She logged in and set hers into a neutral position.

"Might want to borrow one of these," the marine said, tentatively moving a gripping arm back and forth. "Use it in training against my boys and girls. Give them a surprise they won't forget."

"You break it, you bought it."

"Absolutely."

"Your surprise, though—that I'll have to get cleared by the commander."

"Of course."

"Now," Lily said, typing rapidly on her loader's controller, "you should be in learning mode. Just follow the directions."

For twenty minutes the two loaders went through an odd sort of mirror dance as Lily followed and watched every move. By the end, she was pretty sure the marine had got it.

Safing both units, Lily clambered off her unit, while Daniella acrobatically swung free.

"Thanks, ensign—that was fun." The marine offered a hand, which Lily took. It was warm and damp from their exercise.

"My pleasure, lieutenant," Lily said, smiling broadly.

"I'll get back to you on that training gig," Daniella finally said. "So you can get it cleared by your superior."

Lily realized she might've held onto the girl's hand too long. "Uh, sure. My loader rental rates are quite reasonable. Best on board."

"I'll just bet." Daniella winked at her again, smiling brightly. "See ya around."

The Marine officer grabbed her empty water bottle, looped it on her belt, and began to towel off the sweat as she headed out from the cargo bay.

Lily remembered to breathe.

♦♦♦

Staterooms in the officer ranks were assigned by billet, so the Junior Cargo Officer was housed in a Quad with three other ensigns: Starboard Power Officer, Port Inboard Engineering Officer and the Deputy Disaster Recovery Team Manager. The latter, Alicia Morales, had duty, leaving Lily with the two boys in her Quad. As long as they were in port, the boys wanted to go out every night, have some drinks and play some games. They all had to live together, so sometimes Lily went along—thankfully they all kept the easygoing non-confrontational lifestyle each had experienced in the dorms at the Academy. Perhaps there really was method to Fleet's madness regarding roommates.

That's how Lily ended up at Radcliffe's Bar and Pool Hall down on Level 27 with Ron and Bruce. To her dismay—or joy—a gang of young Marine officers had also gathered at Radcliffe's to shoot some pool. Including one particular second lieutenant, happily finishing a cheeseburger between shots. Ron noticed the direction of Lily's gaze.

"So you like the look of the 833rd tonight, huh?"

"It's above average," Lily said casually, trying not to blush at getting caught.

"I sure like watching that second lieutenant shoot," Bruce sighed. "It's worth it no matter which way she bends over."

"She's not in your league," Ron told Bruce.

At that moment Daniella looked up and noticed Lily. She smiled, raising her beer in salute. Flustered, Lily could only do the same. Then to Lily's horror, Daniella started walking over.

"You got that right. I think she might not even be on my team," Bruce laughed and clapped Lily on the shoulder. "Looks like you're up, ensign—make the Navy proud."

The guys tactfully exited towards the pool table, leaving Lily at the bar as Daniella sat down.

"I just thought I'd say thanks again for the lovely dance the other night—with the loaders. A rather unique experience."

"Uh, yeah," Lily managed to say. *This is SO stupid—why am I completely tongue-tied with this…gorgeous woman in front of me trying to make small talk? This is as bad as high school.*

"That and I couldn't help noticing you have a habit of staring in my direction."

"Um…"

"Of course," Daniella said, turning back to her beer, "I must put on quite a show. Your boys just now were looking, too. And the other day with Lt. Walsh."

That's odd. "How do you know Walsh?" Lily asked. "He's not part of the *Mastodon* crew."

Daniella's eyes twitched as if she was caught at something. "Hey—until the other day, I wasn't part of the *Mastodon's* crew either. I know lots of people."

"Right."

"So…where are you from?"

"What, you mean originally?"

"Sure. I'm guessing you didn't come from Chalet Station."

"Minneapolis—it's in Minnesota," Lily said.

"No! I'm from St. Paul."

"New Central High?"

"Nope, Our Lady of the Savior."

"Wow," Lily said, shaking her head. "I can't believe this. Here we are, 343 light years from Earth…"

"…and we grew up just miles away from each other," Daniella said. "And only now are we being formally introduced."

"Lily. Lillian Branoch," she held out a hand. "So pleased to meet you."

"Dani. Daniella Cruz-Ortega. Likewise, I'm sure." This time the handshake was of a more decorous duration.

"Do you like hockey?"

"You mean ice hockey?"

"Is there any other kind?" The two women giggled conspiratorially. Lily was delighted.

"I was captain of my high school's team," Daniella said.

Recognition suddenly struck Lily. "You were the quarterback of the football team, too."

Daniella demurely closed her long eyelashes and bent her head in acknowledgment. "Guilty as charged."

"You beat us 64-0 my junior year."

"Hey—I was the third string quarterback. We tried not to run up the score."

"I hated you."

"And look at us now." Daniella smirked. "A few years later and suddenly you love me."

Lily swallowed hard. *Am I THAT obvious?* "It'll never work out," she finally said aloud.

"What, this whole woman to woman thing?"

"Uh, no," Lily said, backpedaling as fast as she could. "I mean, you're a Marine and I'm Navy and..."

"Oh," Daniella said, nodding sagely. "You mean the whole I'm an officer in the Unified Star Fleet Marine Corps and as such I am supposed to be ready to deploy anywhere in zero time? So how can one even think of starting a relationship when I could be ordered away on a moment's notice—and at the whim of my superior officers? You mean that one?"

"Yeah," Lily said, embarrassed to find herself blushing. "It sounds stupid, doesn't it?"

"Yeah, it does," Daniella said, standing up. "Especially when you haven't even asked about this woman to woman thing—and you don't even know if I'm interested in women. I'll see you later."

Lily actually felt sick. *How can I be such an idiot?*

◆◆◆

Returning to the *Mastodon's* dock, Lily saw a weapons pallet bot gliding down the ramp as she walked up. She thought nothing of it at first, still going over and over her encounter with Daniella, wanting to really kick herself for blurting out her latest doubts. Then she realized the man in the service jumpsuit accompanying the bot was Lt. Walsh, though he showed no signs of knowing who she was.

At the check-in podium she signed herself back in, then casually asked the duty chief, "Lt. Walsh from the *Overton*—what was he doing here?"

The chief glanced at his databoard. "Delivery screw up. His manifest said deliver two pallets to us—we're full up. Got our weapons delivery yesterday."

"I know," Lily said. "Thanks."

She was almost to the triple-airlock which led into the forward section of the ship when it hit her. Why would a lieutenant accompany a delivery of just two pallets after hours? Something wasn't right and Lily found herself going the other way towards Cargo Bay 12.

Standing in the middle corridor of the small compartment surrounded by weapons pallets, she didn't know what she was looking for. A databoard provided no documentation that Walsh had been here. And yet . . .

One of the stacks of weapons pallets didn't look right. She checked the databoard again—the correct number of pallets appeared in the inventory. Not satisfied, she pulled her own datapad from her belt holster slot and ran it against the databoard. Almost immediately she had it—M620 long-range grenade rounds. Both sets of records said there'd been 240 rounds delivered. But while the databoard said these were in twelve pallets, her datapad had scanned the bar codes of fourteen unique pallet IDs when they'd been checked in.

Okay, so she'd been distracted for a minute back then—blushing slightly at the memory of covertly watching Daniella do her chin-ups—but she had fourteen distinctly valid bar codes. She'd clearly scanned something. And the two extra codes didn't match any of the rest of Cargo Bay 12's inventory.

It was late. Waking people up right now would have the

wrong people higher up asking all sorts of questions. She put a seal on this bay and scheduled an inventory inspection first thing in the morning. And gave herself time to find another explanation.

◆◆◆

Opening weapons pallets and verifying their contents required properly trained personnel—Marines—to do the handling. Lily had Chief Armande make the request to the Marine detachment. Immediately she had five Marines carefully opening every pallet and inspecting the contents.

They started with the dozen pallets of M620 long-range grenade rounds, then worked on pulse rifle charge packs. Halfway through that task Daniella showed up in Cargo Bay 12.

"Ensign Branoch," Daniella said. "I didn't know you had authority over any of my men."

"I don't, lieutenant," Lily replied, with equal formality. "What I can do is make a request of your colonel to provide troops trained in handling weapons."

"Ah. Understandable."

"And how did you get in here anyway? I've secured this cargo bay—and I do have the authority for that."

"These are my men," Daniella said, a slight edge creeping into her voice. "They had no order to exclude their supervising officer."

"Not that you are unwelcome here," Lily quickly replied.

"So what's this op about?"

"Probably nothing," Lily said. "But the supply ship *Overton* tried sending over two weapons pallets last night for items we've already received. Since this is my area, I thought I'd better make a complete inventory of the military supplies before I reported to my bosses that the *Overton* had screwed up."

"In other words, you get my men up early to cover your ass?" Daniella's questions was asked with a humorous twinkle in her eye. And a slight downward glance.

Lily had to wonder, did she just check out my ass? Unable to keep from smiling, she answered as best she could. "Um, actually it's so you wouldn't find yourselves two pallets shy of a full weapons load in a fight."

"Ah, now that's an op I can get behind. What can I do to help?"

With two officers supervising, the rest of the inspection took hardly any time.

"So it looks like the *Overton* is full of crap then," Daniella said, as the last of the Marines returned to the barracks and the heavy doors to Cargo Bay 12 clanged shut. "Case closed."

"Yeah," Lily had to agree.

"Know anybody over there? Any candidates in your fraternity of cargo officers who might not be able to add two plus two?"

"Yeah. I mean, not that I know him. But I know of a candidate."

"There you are then," Daniella said, pulling off her work gloves and stowing them in a utility pocket. "Oh, and thanks for looking out for my men. I get a little touchy sometimes with people ordering Marines around for little shit details—I'm supposed to be the one ordering the little shit details. But you were right to make sure the inventory matches the manifest."

"Buy you lunch?" Lily asked.

"No, sorry," Daniella said, stepping back towards the hatch. "I've got security duty—I'll be enjoying my lunch sealed up in my armor."

"Another time, maybe?"

"Maybe."

And with that the Marine lieutenant was gone, leaving Lily alone in Cargo Bay 12, surrounded by all the weapons and munitions she'd signed for—less the two pallets she couldn't account for.

◆◆◆

The inventory check showed nothing missing and Lily's own datapad showed two pallets gone—they couldn't both be right, so once back in Cargo Control she called up the security cam records for Cargo Bay 12.

Movement outside the windows made Lily look up. Three armored Marines were entering the hangar bay. One had second lieutenant's bars—probably Daniella, though all black armor looked the same. Meanwhile, the records tiled across Lily's console screens.

The first cam showed nothing on quick-scan. Neither did the second. But Lily knew there was a third cam, one that had been reported for intermittent transmission problems when she first joined the *Mastodon*. Typical of the disposable sensor culture in Fleet, Security had just installed another cam. It took a couple of minutes to find the maintenance record and locate the ID link address for the old cam. When she did, it was clear the unit was still in operation.

The quick-scan, which looked for changes between frames, paused at 2117 hours when someone entered Cargo Bay 12. Lily blinked twice before rechecking the previous records—there were no changes reported by either of the other cams at 2117 hours Ship Time. She resumed playback.

A second figure came into the bay, Walsh with his weapons pallet bot. Unfortunately, the position of the cam and the stacks of pallets meant she couldn't see what they were doing. Maybe it was innocent—after all the duty chief at the check-in podium recorded that Lt. Walsh had left with his original load.

But who was the other person? Lt. Walsh had no standing on her ship and certainly no authority to enter her secured cargo bay. And there was no paperwork Lily could find signed by any of her chiefs or her supervisor.

Then she got a clear view of the other person and froze the frame. There was no doubt—it was USFMC 2nd Lt. Daniella

Cruz-Ortega. Someone who definitely did not have authority to be in that cargo bay at that hour, unsupervised, and couldn't have signed Lt. Walsh's paperwork.

How could they not appear on the other two cams? These were supposed to be the raw feeds—they still had all their security codes intact. Later, after the records were at least a month old, the files would be compressed to save only the differences between frames. Someone had altered the records from the two known cams. Someone who understood security procedures and had access to a program that could make changes without altering the security codes.

Fleet was well aware that digital records could be altered, and they swore up and down that their security systems made it impossible to tamper with the files. A whole culture of trust in Fleet data had been built up.

Either she'd made some fundamental error, which seemed doubtful, or something nefarious was going on way above her pay grade. And it seemed to involve the beautiful Daniella.

Along with her datapad's inventory, Lily saved her findings on two additional data cards and had them sealed—one by the bosun's mate and one by the ship's clerk. By themselves, these steps weren't unusual, except that Lily rarely had need for duplicate security measures.

Feeling a little sick to her stomach, Lily realized that her own activities were beginning to look suspicious. She needed to solve this problem and quickly. But how?

◆◆◆

Some hours later it occurred to Lily that if Lt. Walsh hadn't taken any of the signed-for inventory, perhaps something else was involved. When all the pallets came aboard, none of them were actually opened and inspected. She'd merely taken Fleet at their word that sealed weapons pallets, kept under positive Fleet control, would contain what the manifest claimed.

But what if this was a dodge of some sort? If you were

trying to steal Fleet supplies—or God help them—smuggle drugs or other contraband, putting two false pallets aboard the *Mastodon* and then removing them later under the cover of a clerical error might be fairly effective.

So where were the two pallets?

She ran a security analysis package against one viddie frame of Lt. Walsh in the hangar bay. The error bars on the measurements weren't conclusive, but the two pallets carried on the transfer bot he escorted might've been a centimeter larger than the weapons pallets. Empty shells brought aboard to cover the two missing pallets?

Since all weapons pallets had tracking tags, Lily took a chance and searched for her missing pallets. They didn't show up in this ship after being delivered to Cargo Bay 12, but to her surprise there was a record of them leaving the ship—the timestamp matched when Lily saw Lt. Walsh. The powerful pulse scanners in the pylons set up at the ship's threshold to the docking ramp must've detected the hidden pallets.

She'd been assuming that Lt. Walsh had returned to the *Overton*, but instead station records tracked him to Chalet Station's civilian Central Storage facility—a warehouse not under Fleet control. There the trail went cold.

Then Lily realized the station system simply wouldn't supply the information. *Two can play this game*, she thought. Typing rapidly, Lily established herself as the owner of the contraband and the Central Storage facility cheerfully coughed up the data. The two bar codes for the false pallets were still registered there.

Lily took a deep breath. She needed to get to the bottom of this. Wearing a Fleet uniform into a civilian cargo facility wasn't considered good policy. But as the Junior Cargo Officer, Lily had the right to go aboard the station and visit their Central Storage—just not in the middle of the day.

◆◆◆

Lying on her bunk, Lily stared up at the darkness and kept wishing she didn't like Daniella. Only aboard for a few days with the 833rd and she was already involved in a major security breach? There had to be a simple explanation. Unless the girl was dirty. She had to put Daniella out of her thoughts.

At 0212 hours Ship Time, Lily left her stateroom and made her way to Cargo Control. From a locker, Lily got a nondescript gray jumpsuit that easily went over her uniform. She wrinkled her nose at its rank smell. Fleet offered much better water rationing than most spacers got—Lily showered at least once a day. Perhaps the odor from this jumpsuit would cover up the fact Lily smelled too good to be wandering around dark places. A station ball cap that'd been left on one of the consoles completed the ensemble. She slipped on a pair of dataglasses and activated the cam, linking it to her datapad.

Signing off the ship at this hour seemed an acceptable risk. Cargo officers were well known for deals made for odd supplies with some of the seamier denizens of station life, though Ensign Lily Branoch had never before been logged for such an operation. The chief manning the podium didn't seem to think anything was out of the ordinary.

Security at Central Storage, even at this late hour, was as lax as she could imagine. Nothing but a small screen and keypad on the hatch—all it wanted was a bar code, which she could supply. The system displayed the aisle number and opened the hatch.

The overhead lighting came on in front of Lily. There were hundreds of cargotainers shelved here. Taking a deep breath, then slowly letting it out, Lily began to search for the right pallets.

They weren't there.

None of the cargotainers looked the right shape either; though Lt. Walsh had already hidden pallets inside pallets—perhaps he'd done it again.

She went up and down Aisle 10 twice, then started to check Aisle 9 when she heard a noise behind her. Nothing had changed in Aisle 10, but in Aisle 11 she could see something sticking out from one of the shelves. Though covered with some sort of spray-on white foam insulation, the material didn't cover the bar codes of the two weapons pallets and her datapad confirmed that these were the right code numbers.

Her right hand brushed against the second pallet as she scanned them, leaving a white mark. The white foam was still damp. That noise she heard—someone had to be here.

The lights shut off.

In the dark, Lily pressed a key on her datapad to update the link. She didn't know which way to go—she was unarmed and had no one backing her up. If she survived this, Lily could imagine her superiors questioning her judgment and right now, she'd have to agree with them.

The cam built into her dataglasses had limited low-light and infrared capacity, enough so she could adjust the glasses to overlay a picture on the otherwise opaque darkness ahead. She'd just taken a step towards the way out when she saw movement ahead at the far end of the aisle. Spinning around she was confronted by a second figure in a shooting stance only a few meters away, aiming what had to be a weapon in her direction.

"Halt!" Lt. Daniella Cruz-Ortega bellowed as the lights came back on. "You're under arrest!"

If the Marine officer hadn't been holding a pulse pistol, Lily might've laughed. As it was, the sight of Daniella in unmarked black soft armor padding in the middle of this compromising situation made Lily almost sick, but it had to be played through to the end. She was so close to solving the mystery of this crime against Fleet.

Raising her hands in surrender, Lily spoke with more assurance than she felt. "And for what charges could you possibly be arresting me, *lieutenant*?"

"Stealing Fleet munitions."

"You're accusing me of stealing?"

"You're listed as the Owner-of-Record of these crates. And understand, *ensign*, that all statements you make can and will be examined as a part of this investigation."

"Prove to me that these are Fleet munitions—when there's nothing missing from my cargo bay—and then explain how they got here in this warehouse before I signed for them."

"I am not at liberty to discuss the particulars of this case," Daniella said.

"She's still got those dataglasses recording," Lt. Walsh warned.

"Turn them off, Ensign Branoch."

"You don't want to do that," Lily said.

"I'm not requesting or arguing with you," Daniella said. "I'm ordering you."

"All right," Lily said, touching the right temple piece. "But the end of that data stream means my recordings have just been automatically forwarded to the bosun's mate and the third officer."

"Give me that datapad!" Daniella ordered. She stepped forward and reached out with one hand. After glancing at the datapad, Daniella flipped it to Lt. Walsh. "What the hell's going on here?"

"I have you right here where you're not supposed to be," Lily said, "with pallets that don't exist."

"Wait," Daniella said, pulling her hands back and pointing the barrel of the pulse pistol towards the ceiling, "you're investigating us?"

"Your fingerprints were recorded on pallets in Cargo Bay 12 and I suspect they'll be on these pallets."

"Of course my fingerprints are on the pallets. I assisted in your inspection."

"You were wearing gloves, lieutenant."

"Barely even circumstantial, ensign."

"I have security cam evidence that you and Lt. Walsh transferred two weapons pallets in Cargo Bay 12 to these two dummy pallets the other night."

"Sweet Jesus!" Daniella swore. "Walsh, you said you fixed the security cam records."

"I did."

"You missed the third cam," Lily said, unable to keep a trace of a smile from her face. "I saw Lt. Walsh leaving the ship at a time when he shouldn't have been there. And I saw the two of you in Cargo Bay 12, which was sealed at the time—you shouldn't have been there either. The two of you are stealing Fleet supplies."

"This isn't what it seems," Daniella said.

"Really?" Lily was beginning to feel vindicated. "So what would I find if I opened this?"

"Do you mean you don't know?" Walsh asked, sounding relieved.

"No."

"This is a classified operation."

"Right. Fleet weapons in a civilian storage facility."

"Actually," Walsh said, "it happens a lot more often than you know. Fleet has many undercover operations which cannot be supplied directly by Fleet sources."

"Undercover?" Lily asked. "This whole mess is the result of some misguided cloak-and-dagger operation? What is this, amateur hour?"

"Shit," Daniella swore more forcefully this time. "Walsh, you said you do this all the time. I was brought in specifically to help you because no one knew me on this ship. Let's get out of here and finish this on the ship."

"That's not going to happen," Lily said.

"Sounds like there are going to be more people coming in a

few minutes," Walsh said sadly. "Cover's blown on this op."

"Am I still under arrest?" Lily said.

"No," Daniella said, holstering her weapon. In the distance they all heard the hatch to Central Storage opening. "We're all down here! Aisle 11, gentlemen."

❖❖❖

The next two days were best described as Classified. Walsh showed up for a closed session the first day, but no one had seen him since. Lily had been required to present her testimony and findings to a series of senior and command officers, both from the *Mastodon* and other Fleet ships in port at Chalet Station. Her judgment had been questioned regarding not bringing this up with her superiors before trying to go "all cowboy" and "round up the criminals" on her own. In the end, she'd been advised that she might earn Fleet's unwanted consolation prize for such miscalculations—the Devotion To Duty medal.

It'd been hard to get back to the ordinary work of loading cargo.

Senior Chief Armande repeated himself in his distinctive working class Toronto accent. "We've got sixty-two tonnes of whole wheat flour coming aboard tomorrow bound for the Fleet Stores at BR-72. They're one-tonne vacuum-compacted shipping blocks and certified vermin-free. I need your permission to load them in Cargo Bay 4."

"Why Four? It's not a big load…"

"Because BR-72 is our next port of call and the X.O. doesn't want it buried in the back."

"Oh. Right—that makes sense," Lily said, approving the move. "Sorry about before. I was just distracted for a moment."

"It's been more than a moment, sir."

"Excuse me?"

"Ensign, are you going to ask that cute Marine lieutenant out? It's gonna be a lot harder when we head out into space if you don't."

"What do you know?" Lily asked, mortified that he wasn't talking about the investigation.

"Come on, ensign. I'm a senior chief petty officer. Chiefs run the ship—we know everything that's going on. And what we don't know, we've got Marine sergeants in the Corps who can tell us."

"Oh God." Lily sighed.

"Just ask her," Armande urged. "For all our sakes."

"What if she says no?"

"Happens all the time," Armande said. "And anyway, how is that worse than where you are now, sir? You don't supervise each other and you're both officers so the fraternization rules don't apply."

"Lt. Cruz-Ortega is a Marine—she can be transferred at any time."

Chief Armande laughed. "Now you're making excuses. The woman just got here with the 833rd. I doubt she'll be asked to leave before the weekend, let alone our departure date. Seems to me, after your little black ops skullduggery, you two ought to sit down and have a helluva good laugh about all this. But if you don't ask, you'll never know."

"When did you get to be so wise, chief?"

"Don't know that I am, sir. I do know that having my immediate superior officer moping around makes my life more difficult no matter what I personally think. And Chalet isn't the worst space station in West Space to have dinner and a night out with a pretty girl. Especially compared to a garden spot like BR-72 and later out in The Fringe."

"True. Thanks, chief."

"Don't mention it. Really—don't mention it."

◆◆◆

But in the end Lily hadn't managed to call that night. In the morning she sat by herself picking at her breakfast, when

Lt. Cruz-Ortega appeared holding her own tray.

"Mind if I join you?" Daniella asked.

"Um…no mind at all," Lily said, wincing at the awkward words stumbling out of her mouth. "Look, I'm sorry about…"

"Truce?"

"Sure." Lily smiled. "Truce."

Daniella took her place across from Lily. While salting and peppering her two over-easy eggs next to a stack of pancakes, she said, "You're staring at that datapad like it might burst into flames."

"Messages from Earth."

"Problem?"

"My mother doesn't understand me. Never has."

"Only your mother?" Daniella seemed amused, starting on her pancakes. "Not your father?"

"Oh, my father is disappointed with me because he doesn't believe in star travel. It's the 29th century and I'm supposed to stay in Minnesota. What about your family?"

"Marines are sort of like the family business. My biggest problem is my oldest brother who is pissed off that I made officer straight off instead of coming up through the ranks."

"Isn't he proud of you?"

"Sure—but he's loads older and we're both the same rank. Bruises his manly ego." She paused to shovel in the last two large bites of pancake before washing it down with some coffee.

Lily's own breakfast had mainly been rearranged on her plate, but she managed to take another bite of toast.

"When are you finally going to get around to asking me out?" Daniella asked, looking at her expectantly, holding her nearly empty coffee cup with both hands.

Lily took a deep breath. "I was thinking after breakfast."

"Seems like a long time to wait." There was that cocked eyebrow again, waiting for Lily.

"Dani—would you like dinner on the station tonight?"

"Just dinner?"

"My time is free after that."

"You don't have some of that important naval officer shit duty to pull?"

"Not for forty-eight hours."

Daniella raised an eyebrow. "Forty-eight? I kind of like the sound of that."

"What about your tough gyrene show of power duties?"

"I can take a forty-eight if I want."

"So?" Lily pressed for an answer. "I can get us a table at Rembrandt's on Level 2—best steak dinner in a hundred light years. Or so I'm told. I haven't actually been there before. Not the sort of place one goes alone."

"Uniforms?"

"I won't if you won't," Lily said.

Daniella smiled at this and said, "Then I might just wear high heels."

Lily blushed and stared back down at her datapad.

"You going to read your messages from your mom?" Daniella asked.

"Not right now," Lily said.

But she knew how her next reply to her mother might begin. *Mom, I met a girl.*

Cupcake

Erin MacKay

Today marked the start of the third week of the heat wave in the labor district. Budget cuts at climate control, or layoffs, or water shortages—Admin always had plenty of excuses but never a plan to fix the problem. Stasya sat on a bench in a park at ground level, where the heat was worse but privacy easier to find. Dressed in the same gray pants and shirt as everyone else in the park, she looked like one more worker taking an early supper break beneath the artificial lights of the skydome. But her bento box lay beside her on the bench, unopened, and cupped in her hands she held a piece of technology a bit beyond the reach of most members of the service caste.

Leaning forward, elbows resting on her knees, Stasya studied the small screen of her handheld, scrolling through the photos with increasing dismay.

"You're kidding, right, Rupi? This is your idea of a joke."

Rupi's laughter crackled through her earpiece. "No joke, babe. By the end of the week."

"But she's just a...a cupcake," Stasya sputtered.

"She's a cupcake with a corporate life insurance policy and a husband who's looking at bankruptcy and hostile takeover."

Stasya closed the photo file and Rupi's plump face filled the screen. For all his previous mirth, he was watching her a little too carefully. "Bad luck for her. Any other instructions?"

"Make it look like an accident."

"What's the catch, Rupi?" Stasya tucked a wayward strand of hair behind her ear. "You can do this piece of fluff for a lot cheaper than me."

Rupi's mouth shriveled just before his face disappeared, replaced by an e-mail encryption emblem. "Here's the file on her security."

Stasya opened it as soon as the download finished. She flicked through the information, then blinked and went through it again, more slowly. "Holy..."

"You see? Getting close to her is going to take some doing. Not everyone on my roster is up to it."

Stasya grunted agreement, still scrolling through the security manifest. Most of the names on it she recognized as agents of expensive firms who specialized in corporate caste protection. A woman headed up the detail, and Stasya strained to remember whether she'd run into this 'Frances' before or not. "One thing I don't get."

Rupi snorted. "Let me guess: How's a husband with a debt the size of the imperial budget afford that kind of muscle?"

"And why would he hire them to protect a woman he's going to knock off?"

"It's paid for by her daddy. Rich daddy."

"Interesting daddy," Stasya muttered. "If he's got the cash to build a wall around Cupcake but doesn't seem inclined to help his son-in-law out of his jam." Stasya clicked the security file closed to free the screen for the camera feed. She wanted to see Rupi's eyes. "All right."

"All right? You're taking the gig?"

"Yes, I'm taking the gig."

"What do you need? Weapons?"

Stasya's eyes grew unfocused while she thought. "No weapons. Not where I'm going."

Stasya cut the connection and tapped her earpiece off.

Slouching back on the bench, she pulled up the photo files of Mitsuko Jennings-Villega. She was young, of course, and pretty beneath the makeup and trendy designer clothes. If Napoleon Villega had wanted a trophy wife, he'd gotten one. But Mitsuko could not have come cheap. Every photo revealed real animal-skin shoes imported from Earth, jewels mined in the farthest reaches of explored space. Her hair, her nails, her skin, were styled and manicured and displayed to perfection, the way only a woman born to it could pull off. In every shot, Mitsuko was smiling at someone, sometimes laughing. And why not?

Stasya looked up at the cluster of gleaming dome-scrapers that soared up from the gravitational center of the colony. Officially the New Chueca Colonial Enterprises Group, LLC Mixed Use Development, the compound was called High Street by residents and outsiders alike. While the labor district kept water flowing and oxygen pumping through New Chueca's tiny ecosphere, while miners sent robotic bores deep into the asteroid's surface to find gold, platinum, and water, up in the glass mazes of High Street, the men and women of the corporate caste prepared for dinner. In High Street, dinner was not just a meal, it was an event, crystal and champagne, every night. And woe to the woman who made her appearance at any less than her stunning best.

Mitsuko Jennings-Villega would, even now, be surrounded by her attendants: one of them presenting her with a selection of earrings on a velvet-lined tray; another gelling and curling her dark hair into the latest intricate style; yet another putting the finishing touches on a sparkling pedicure. By the time the dome lights went down and New Chueca entered its statutory ten hours of darkness, Mitsuko would be immersed in High Street's shimmering nightlife.

Stasya imagined Mitsuko walking down a hallway, passing vases of fresh flowers, her face illuminated by tiny incandescent lights. High Street had flowers while the people below couldn't afford vegetables, and the warm, flattering ambience of their

world was probably the real reason Admin didn't have any power left to regulate the temperature in the labor district. Stasya's jaw clenched at the thought of going up there again.
She should have asked Rupi for more money.

❖❖❖

Three days and several clandestine arrangements later, Stasya raised her left hand to the scanners, using her trusty service sector I.D. to gain access to High Street's eastern employee checkpoint. Once inside the compound, she made her way to the employee locker room, clanging and crowded with laborers at the shift change. She found her contact easily; in the midst of the activity he was the only person who seemed to have no purpose, neither coming nor going. Nervous, dumpy, wearing his service grays like a costume, he caught her eye and made a fluttering gesture that he must have thought looked surreptitious. She tensed to keep herself from rolling her eyes at Rupi's new talent, and followed the man to the last row of lockers.

He held his hand out, waiting. Stasya pulled out her handheld and punched up the prearranged debit. He glanced at it and nodded, too quickly to have actually scrutinized the amount. Amateur. She scanned his I.D., completing the transfer.

He glanced around, then pressed his hand against the scanpad of the locker to his right. It clicked open. He stepped away from her, but she caught his elbow and held him while she made sure the package was there. She saw Rupi's signature, one short, coarse gray hair tied around the closure of the bag to ensure it had not been opened since leaving his hands. "Perv," she murmured.

She released her jumpy contact and watched him disappear around the corner. Just to make him sweat a little more, she waited a moment before she pulled the bag from the locker and followed him out to the service corridor.

When they reached a line of rolling laundry trolleys, he stopped at one and pushed aside a layer of linens. "Get in," he hissed.

She looked at the soiled sheets and back at him. "You're kidding, right?" Shaking her head, she walked past him to swipe her hand across the call key for the freight elevator. "I'll take it from here."

Alone in the freight elevator, she swiped her hand again and went to the highest floor her I.D. could access. Stasya had never been to this part of High Street. Even the corporate caste considered Zone Six East the high-rent district. Following the map her housekeeping contact had provided the night before, she wound her way down ever smaller and more dimly lit corridors until she found a properly isolated ladies' room. Still in her gray service clothes, she styled her chin-length blonde hair into sculpted waves and applied makeup with a practiced hand.

When the ten-minute warning for lightdown sounded, she pulled off her pants and shirt. Before leaving her flat, she had applied translucent body paint, and now her pale skin danced with glittering opalescence. A short, sleeveless black dress in several filmy layers slid like a whisper over her head; the hem drifting weightlessly around her thighs. Her feet went into high, strappy heels. Last, she draped long strands of jet beads around her neck. They clicked and swung with the slightest movement. She hated formal occasions, the dressing up, the fuss, the impractical adornments. But she especially hated the shoes.

The gray service clothing was recyclable, but she stuffed it down the incinerator chute instead, along with the bag containing the makeup, and enough of her genetic material to provide her real identity to anyone who was interested. Her handheld went into a slim evening clutch. Then she looked in the mirror and pulled on a few last, vital accessories: the affected slouch of a High Street elite, a knowing smirk, and a flirtatious sparkle to hide the habitual vigilance of her green eyes.

While some members of her profession excelled at blending

into the shadows, Stasya had always found that an assassin's best armor was brazenness. If you walked like High Street, talked like High Street, and disdained the rest of humanity like High Street, no one asked any questions. Stasya tapped her hand on the pad at the door and continued into the dining room without breaking stride. The maitre d' opened his mouth to stop her, then closed it as the I.D. pad beeped confirmation and a cultured female voice announced her to whomever might be interested: "Elissa Nakamura, Kyushu Neurogenetics Corporation."

High Street decor had changed with fashion, but the excess remained. The overwrought flower arrangements of her memory had transformed into bamboo and bonsai trees; the dark, glossy mahogany and silver had become subdued birch and river stone. The people who sat around each of the room's twenty-seven tables wore different clothes, different hairstyles, but they still chatted and smiled and convinced each other they were having a good time. If Stasya had held any stake in this fool's pageant, she would have been mortified to be among these people, trying to be one of them. She would have been nervous, said the wrong things to the wrong people, and revealed herself to be an impostor before the soup course.

But the reality was, she just didn't give a damn, and so she pulled it off. When she made small talk with lascivious Assistant Deputy General Managers and their third wives, she garnished the charade with a hint of her very real contempt.

"Yes, a recent transfer from New Ginza, pleasure to meet you," she burbled. "Oh, I arrived two days ago, but it's been just a diamond-edged bitch getting myself on B-Quadrant time. First course already? You don't linger over your cocktails here, do you?"

All the while, she kept her eye on Mitsuko.

Isolated in her photographs, Mitsuko had looked tall, but she proved petite and slender in the company of other humans. She wore a dress that plunged in the back and shimmered with the same hint of gold as her body paint, paired with heels so high she appeared to be walking on her toes like a dancer. Her thick, black hair was elaborately arranged, and Stasya wondered how she supported the weight of it on her tiny neck. The delicate bones of her face reflected her mother's aristocratic blood, but her father's Anglo genes showed in eyes that were a little too light and large. She arrived on the arm of her husband, a man who might have been darkly handsome if he hadn't been racing toward old age decades before his time. He had the skittish eyes of a man so crushed by debt that he had taken out a contract on his own wife.

Clumsy as he was with his finances, Napoleon Villega had his uses tonight. Mitsuko had four bodyguards, dressed in matching black suits, stationed at varying distances from her in the dining room. Three more were mixed in among the serving staff, including one woman. Stasya identified them almost instantly, thanks to the fact that Napoleon kept tagging them with frequent glances. One would think he was planning on killing his wife himself, nervous as he was about those guards.

Through five courses, Stasya barely touched her food—High Street women who ate full meals were suspected of not being able to afford good quality drugs—and hunger joined the long list of reasons for her increasingly foul mood. She looked longingly at the glass of wine she had been wetting her lips with all evening, and promised herself a good, stiff drink after this job was done.

Mitsuko, on the other hand, indulged herself, tossing back several glasses of wine, with enough water in between that Stasya marveled at her endurance. At last, just before the final course, Mitsuko spoke to the waitress refilling her glass, the woman Stasya had already identified as a guard. The waitress nodded, and disappeared down the short hallway that led to the ladies room. A moment later, Mitsuko rose from her chair, laughing and patting the shoulder of the woman beside her at the table.

Finally. Stasya gave Mitsuko a twenty-second head start, then excused herself. Her brain snapped into high gear as she made her way between the tables; her senses hummed with alert concentration. The chatter of the other diners drifted into her awareness and back out again; the flicker of a candle, the sparkle of a lifted glass, the jerk and clink of a chopstick dropped on a tray, were observed and dismissed and left not a ripple of distraction in their wake.

The guard was the key. If she stood outside the door, Stasya could make it could look like an accident—a few drops of water, a slip on those monstrously high heels, an unlucky fall against the granite basin. If the guard had gone in, though, things would be different. Stasya could prevent screaming, if she worked quickly enough. But there would probably be blood.

Well, that was why she wore black tonight.

No one stood outside the ladies' room door. For one grim moment, Stasya wondered if Mitusko's guards were thorough enough to lock the door to a public restroom while Mitusko was inside, but the door slid open as Stasya passed the sensor. The vestibule was larger and more expensively appointed than Stasya's entire apartment. An elderly attendant in a shapeless gray service dress smiled at her, with a welcoming gesture meant to convey her availability for any need Stasya might face. Stasya merely nodded acknowledgement and passed through the next door, into the lavatory.

The guard stood rigidly against the wall beside the sinks, not even trying to affect the sort of casual impatience a real waitress would have exhibited. As she passed, Stasya noted the guard's solid stance and began formulating strategies for the task of getting rid of her. Most of them began with getting the woman's legs out from under her and ended with her head abruptly meeting the marble countertop. Followed by a small transaction to buy the attendant's silence, of course.

Out of five stalls, only one door was closed. Stasya went to the sink and leaned over toward the mirror, making a show of blinking and reaching for a tissue to dab beneath her eye.

"Something in your eye?" the guard asked, her voice a monotone drawl.

Stasya made a sound of affirmation. "As always. I can't get through a night without ruining my makeup."

The guard snorted, not even bothering to feign sympathy.

The stall door opened, and Stasya watched in the mirror as Mitsuko came out. Perhaps it was the brighter light of the lavatory, but Mitsuko didn't look the same as she had in the dining room. The way she held her head betrayed a hint of fatigue, and her plastic smile had gone, replaced by a soft sadness.

Mitsuko rested her hand on the doorframe of the stall, and stared right at Stasya. "It's about time you caught me alone. You've been looking at me all night."

The guard was good. She produced a gun from her service grays so quickly Stasya almost missed the movement. There was no missing the gun trained on her forehead, though.

"Don't even breathe," the guard said.

Adrenaline spiked in Stasya's veins. So, the target was on to her. Or was she? Mitsuko didn't seem frightened.

Stasya stood frozen in place, watching Mitsuko walk toward her, watching her brown eyes and curving lips and her delicate, swaying limbs. Mitsuko approached her not with fear, but with a strange, wistful sort of hunger. She paused, turning back to her guard.

"Frances," Mitsuko purred. "I think you'll be more comfortable in the vestibule."

Frances looked surprised to be addressed, but her gun hand never wavered and her professional stoicism resurfaced almost immediately. "With all respect, ma'am, I don't think so."

Mitsuko stopped in her tracks. Frances could not see the impatient expression that came over Mitsuko's face, but the sudden stiffness of her shoulders, the sharpness of her tone, was unmistakable. "What is your duty, precisely?"

"To protect you from harm, ma'am. At all costs."

"Is it part of your job description," Mitsuko asked, "to report to my husband if I choose to have an affair?"

Frances's jaw clenched before she answered. "No, ma'am." Slowly, Frances lowered the gun, but she did not put it away.

Mitsuko stood so close that Stasya could smell her lily-scented perfume. Mitsuko laid one hand at her waist and slid the other up to cup her jaw. Keeping an eye out for sudden movements from Frances, Stasya took up Mitsuko's invitation. Running her hands over Mitsuko's thin evening gown, she felt for weapons along Mitsuko's back, and when she encountered no resistance, her touch grew bolder, investigating Mitsuko's stomach and breasts.

With the slightest press of her fingers, Mitsuko urged Stasya's head down and put her lips to Stasya's ear. "I know what you are," Mitsuko breathed. "I want to die, just not here."

Stasya could not help a soft gasp of surprise. Suicide-by-assassin was a new one.

"I think you'll be more comfortable in the vestibule, Frances," Mitsuko said again.

"Ma'am, I think you've had too much to drink—"

"Undoubtedly." Mitsuko pressed herself against Stasya and kissed her. For a time, Stasya managed to put a professional wall between herself and the physical sensations, to ignore Mitsuko's lithe body against hers, her warm mouth, her tongue darting out to brush against Stasya's. Then Mitsuko moaned, and though Stasya knew it was for Frances's benefit, the sound had a maddeningly unfair effect on her focus.

"Yes, ma'am," Frances muttered. She might have said something more than that, about giving them some privacy and keeping watch outside. All Stasya knew was that the inside of Mitsuko's mouth tasted like the wine from dinner and that the gold paint detracted not a bit from the softness of her skin.

Somewhere, a million miles away, the bathroom door slid shut. Her lips still brushing Stasya's, Mitsuko breathed out, then in, then out again. At last, she let go. Stasya lifted her head and watched her take a step back, but it was another moment before Mitsuko opened her eyes.

When Stasya spoke, her voice came out just the way she wanted it, steady, with a hint of coolness. "You want to die."

"Yes." Her eyes flickered away from Stasya's inquiring gaze. "I hope you're good; I'd hate to think Napoleon skimped on me at the end."

Stasya refused to be impressed by Mitsuko's matter-of-fact delivery. She arched an eyebrow and leaned against the sink. "And you knew me, how?"

"Practice makes perfect. You're the third assassin he's hired; the only one who's gotten this close to me. You're very convincing; I would never have guessed you weren't born in High Street."

Stasya bit back an acerbic reply. "Thanks."

Mitsuko's mouth tried to smile but gave up with the job half done. "So, we should go somewhere else to do this. We've been here too long, anyway. You'd never get away now if I identified you."

Stasya hesitated. She wanted to go with Mitsuko, to see what could make a woman kiss her own death with such passion. Yet, there was every reason to think she might be walking into a trap. A strange trap, to be sure, but one never knew.

Mitsuko interpreted her silence correctly. "You don't trust me."

"You can imagine why."

"What if I offer to double whatever you're being paid?"

Stasya grinned. "I'm being paid an awful lot."

Mitsuko sauntered toward her, seduction in every movement. Stasya kept the cynical grin on her face, just to let Mitsuko know she was on to her wiles. But when Mitsuko slid a hand into the neckline of Stasya's dress, her lips parted in spite of herself.

"I'm rich," Mitsuko whispered. Warm fingers curved around Stasya's breast, brushed over the nipple, squeezed just enough. "Very, very rich."

When Stasya opened her eyes and realized her hand had drifted up into Mitsuko's hair, she knew what she was going to say next.

So did Mitsuko. She laid a gentle kiss on Stasya's collarbone, then stood back and waited.

Stasya sighed and straightened. "I'm Elissa."

Mitsuko tilted her head, and while her eyes stayed flat and still, the rest of her transformed back into an ebullient High Street princess. "Elissa, love, do come back to my suite for a nightcap. I want to hear all about New Ginza and the latest fashions there. We get so little innovation in this backwater colony."

Stasya slipped her own High Street persona back into place. "Of course, darling. You're far too kind."

Mitsuko took Stasya's hand and they reentered the dining room laughing like schoolgirls. On the way through the vestibule, Stasya caught Frances's eye and gave the poor, befuddled woman a wink.

◆◆◆

Napoleon stayed late with the men, drinking and smoking cigars and, of course, playing a few hands of cards. Stasya had to wonder how he kept finding games when he was so far in debt. News like that didn't stay a secret for long.

Mitsuko kept one small hand wrapped around Stasya's wrist as if she were afraid that Stasya would change her mind. She waited for a black-suited guard to precede her, then pulled

Stasya along to the lift, leaving a second guard to bring up the rear. Stasya prickled at having an armed man behind her, and once inside the close quarters of the lift, had to resist the urge to jockey with him for a better position.

The first guard tapped his I.D. against the pad and the lift began to move. Mitsuko regaled Stasya with a long, sordid story about one of their dinner companions. High Street considered vicious gossip an art form, and Mitsuko had certainly mastered it. Mitsuko was still chattering when they followed the guards into the Villega suite.

To Stasya's immense relief, the guards left them at the entrance to Mitsuko's private rooms. Mitsuko continued her story as they settled into the low, soft cushions of her sitting room, and all the way through the arrival of a maidservant with a tray of liqueur in a crystal decanter and two delicate, tulip-shaped cordial glasses. "That will be all," Mitsuko told her.

The woman nodded and silently departed. "Lock," Mitsuko called as the door hissed shut. The lock chimed, and Mitsuko fell silent for the first time since leaving the restroom.

Stasya was already starting to recognize the changes that came over Mitsuko when the mask fell off. This time, a deep sigh accompanied it. For a moment, Mitsuko tilted her head back, sinking farther into the cushion. Her cordial glass hung from her fingers, so loose Stasya braced herself for it to fall.

"I want out," Mitsuko said, her voice low and soft.

Stasya reached for her own glass of ruby liqueur and held it up to let the golden lighting of the room shine through it. "Out?"

Mitsuko lifted her head, looked Stasya in the eyes. "Out of here. I want out of High Street, out of this marriage, out of this life. I'm finished. All I want now is to make sure it's done right."

"Understandable. There are easier ways, you know."

Mitsuko shook her head. "You only think that."

"No, I know that. Divorce."

"My first thought, too, but Napoleon refused to give me one. He has my inheritance to think of. He'd fight me all the way." Mitsuko gave Stasya a grim look. "And you know how divorce lawyers are."

Stasya had to take a breath before she could force her jaws apart to reply. "Yes. Yes, I know all about divorce lawyers." She sipped at her liqueur and let it sit on her tongue until it burned before she swallowed it. "Would your father help?

Mitsuko laughed, shallow and bitter. "My father? You obviously don't understand the relationship between fathers and daughters here. And, through some rather convoluted legal instruments, the shares of Napoleon's company I got in the marriage contract are now held by the Jennings Family Partnership—meaning, of course, they're part of Daddy's corporate assets. They go back to Napoleon if I divorce him, per the prenup—a significant loss for Daddy. No help from that direction."

"So run away."

"Where would I go that one of them couldn't track me down? Besides, I've tried. Several times."

"And?"

"You noticed the guards, right? I didn't always have that many. And, I discovered that Napoleon has a…a mean streak, when it comes to his pride. Lucky for me, I can afford good make-up. And good booze." She tipped her head back and downed the rest of her liqueur, swallowing it slowly, her eyes half-lidded. "I think it was the last time I tried that precipitated Napoleon's interest in contract killing. For once, our needs converged."

Stasya stared into her glass, thinking. This assignment was turning into something she wasn't sure she wanted to touch. She should bid Mitsuko good night, refund Rupi's advance, and run like hell. But 'should' and 'should not' were concepts her brain was having a hard time with tonight. For instance, she should not be pointing out alternatives to suicide to her target. Sort of detracted from the whole process of killing her.

Not that inconvenient facts like that were stopping her, not tonight. "So why did you marry him? Corporate matches can be tough, but even the traditionalists give their kids a choice."

"Choice. Interesting word." Mitsuko reached for the decanter and refilled her glass. "I could have said no to Napoleon. Then my father would have presented me with another suitor, and I could have said no to that one, and to the one after that. There comes a point, though, when you can't say no anymore. Not if you ever want to see the light of day again. Pretty daughters are a corporate asset, Elissa, and that's what 'choice' is, to us."

She sipped her liqueur with more decorum than before, her eyes lowered. "I loved him. Or I thought I did. He was charming and handsome—he's still handsome, you have to admit." A shy smile crossed her mouth and Stasya granted her a small one in return. "And he was better than the four other proposals Daddy got when I came of age. He looked me in the eye when he talked to me, as if I were real. When your options are sharks, slime balls and sadists, a gambler starts to look pretty good. I thought I'd made the right decision."

"What happened?"

Mitsuko shook her head. "I don't know. I came back from dinner one night and I suddenly realized I hated all this. Everything my life is—all it's ever been. All the fakery and façades, the drugs, the gossip, the fashion and money and…waste. It's all nonsense. I'm a pawn, an ornament, a body and an investment portfolio. I looked at the busboy and realized he was happier than I am. He goes home at night to his labor district apartment and his service caste wife and his service caste kids, and they eat simple food and they talk to each other and they sleep soundly and they're happy."

"They're not as happy as you think," Stasya said, her voice

flat. "You're being naïve. You've never tasted that life."

"Have you?" Mitsuko looked genuinely curious. "What about you? What's your story?"

Stasya stiffened and set her glass down with deliberate care. That question, depending upon the context, ranged from annoying to dangerous. "My story is that there are choices. It just depends on what you're willing to do."

"Then you understand me," Mitsuko said, leaning forward. "I'm just making one more choice."

Stasya stared at her. She did understand her, and it was not a feeling she liked. "You really want me to kill you."

"I really do. You're a professional; you've done this before, right?"

Stasya nodded. Mitsuko didn't need to know any more details than that.

"So, you can do it right, can't you? Quick?"

"Quick, yes. Painless, too, if that's what you want."

"Yes, that's it." She reached out and brushed her fingers across the back of Stasya's hand, feather-light. Stasya's skin tingled.

"Did you have anything in particular in mind? Your husband wanted it to look like an accident."

"Of course he does. My assets would do him no good if he were suspected of murder, and suicide voids the policy. I don't have any idea how to do it. That's why I need you."

Stasya drained her glass and settled back into the cushions. "Then I need to think."

Mitsuko nodded. "You should stay here tonight. Get some sleep if you want. We don't have to hurry. I'm not going anywhere."

"Yeah." Stasya was already too deep in thought to bother with elegance. Mitsuko said something about a shower, then Stasya was alone in the silence and the lingering scent of lilies.

An hour later, Mitsuko stood at the glass door to the balcony, gazing at the twinkling lights of the surrounding High Street structures. Her damp hair flowed in smooth layers down her back; her delicate features, reflected in the glass, glowed clean and almost childlike. She drew the folds of her silk dressing gown more tightly around her and turned toward Stasya. "Are you still thinking?"

Stasya shook her head slowly. "Do you trust me?"

"Yes."

Stasya's eyebrows lifted at the speed of her reply. "I don't think an accident is the way to go. Any accident a woman like you is likely to encounter in a safe place like High Street would have to be gruesome and painful in order to be fatal. Electrocution, concussion, drowning, poisoning…" She didn't have to continue; Mitsuko gave a visible shudder at the implications.

"Murder is better?"

"I can be more open about it so it can be quick. But the set-up will take more time. We have to establish a relationship; give me some kind of motivation. If it appears the least bit random they'll assume it was a hit and Napoleon will be the first place they'll look."

Mitsuko walked slowly from the window. "Isn't that risky for you?"

"A little. I have certain resources at my disposal that can ensure I get off-colony in a timely and discreet manner. And your husband is paying me well enough that I can buy whatever I don't already have."

"All right." Mitsuko sank down to her knees to sit *seiza* on the floor in front of Stasya. "What kind of relationship?"

Stasya leaned forward and brushed a fingertip down the line of Mitsuko's jaw. "The kind worth murdering over." Flicking her finger off Mitsuko's chin, she smiled.

◆◆◆

Stasya stayed up long after Mitsuko had gone to bed, until she felt comfortable that she had the workings of a plan in her mind.

Cupcake

Only then did she let her drowsiness lead her to the bedroom.

Stasya stood at the end of the bed and watched Mitsuko as she slept, her small form huddled in a ball on one side of the mattress. Stasya couldn't see her face for all the inky hair spilling across it. For an instant, the memory came to her of a zoo on Jin Myung, and a fox, covered in red fur, sleeping nose to tail in the corner of its cage. Stasya had stood in front of the cage for a long time, but the fox had stayed fast asleep. Dreaming of sunlight, perhaps, or rain.

The curled fingers of Mitsuko's hand jerked and Stasya wondered what she was dreaming.

Shaking herself, Stasya resumed her path toward the bathroom, stripping off clothes and shoes as she went. She indulged herself in a long, steaming shower, an extravagance only High Street denizens could afford. Water and shampoo dissolved the stiff waves in her hair; makeup and body paint swirled down the drain. She left the bathroom wrapped in a fluffy towel, deliciously relaxed and drowsy.

She considered rifling through Mitsuko's closet for something to put on, then shrugged and slid into the bed naked. Mitsuko sighed and rolled toward her, blinking awake. "Hm. I like you better clean," she murmured.

"So do I. Go back to sleep. It's late."

"Where did you go?"

Stasya laid a finger over Mitsuko's lips. "You trust me, remember?"

Mitsuko nodded. Stasya lay down on her side, allowing herself to luxuriate in the soft pillow and the velvety, cool sheets. It didn't take long for a sleepy lassitude to creep over her limbs, and her eyes drifted closed.

Stasya's internal clock woke her at lightup, even before the window began de-clouding to gradually let the daylight into the room. Mitsuko still slept, but she had curled away from Stasya during the night. She didn't stir, even when the light grew strong enough to stream over her face and between the strands of hair to reach her eyes. Stasya sighed. They needed to talk, before the parade of servants and guards and social callers began. She laid a hand on Mitsuko's shoulder and shook her.

Nothing. Stasya shook her harder and Mitsuko rewarded her with a low grunt of resistance. "Come on, princess, up and at 'em." She could not help but chuckle a little as she shook Mitsuko again. "Not a morning person, eh?"

Another sound, this one longer and higher, a genuine whine. But her limbs contracted and her body splayed and arched in an involuntary stretch.

The laugh died in Stasya's throat.

It was a long time before she could force her gaze back up to Mitsuko's eyes. She found them open, watching her. "You like?" Mitsuko whispered, her voice rough with the remnants of sleep.

Stasya licked her lips. "Doesn't matter if I like. You're a dead woman, remember?"

The slightest pout formed on her mouth. "I remember." She sat up and yawned, and Stasya drew back into herself on her own side of the bed. "So, what's the plan?"

"You don't need to know the plan," Stasya said shortly. She leaned forward over her knees and touched her toenail where the polish had chipped. "I'll do it sometime over the next few days. If I catch you completely by surprise, you may not even know what hit you."

"Fast and painless," Mitsuko said. "Just like you promised."

"Fast and painless."

"Won't Napoleon get impatient? You're supposed to do it soon, right?"

"Don't worry about Napoleon. He'll get what he paid for."

Mitsuko sat silently for a moment, and Stasya felt the prickle of being watched. "What do we do until then?"

"We keep the masks on. Not a crack, not if this is going to work."

Mitsuko sighed. "That's easy enough."

♦♦♦

Stasya had to try on three of Mitsuko's dresses before she found one stretchy enough to hide how small it was on her tall frame. She was stuck with the shoes she had worn the night before, the mere thought of which was enough to make her feet ache. She made a mental note to put the shoe department first on their list of errands today.

Mitsuko let her maids dress her and sat placidly while they tended to hair and makeup carefully orchestrated for daytime. As a guest, Stasya was expected to make use of Mitsuko's hired help, but she performed as much of her own dressing chores as she could without risking remark. Having strangers flutter and fuss over her tended to make her violent.

They sat at the small cafe table on Mitsuko's balcony for breakfast. Stasya ate with mechanical efficiency, then tapped her foot with impatience while Mitsuko lingered over her tea.

Mitsuko stared out over the rail, not at the labor district below, which had been awake and functioning for hours, but at the skydome, the frosty, white-lit shield that separated them from the airless darkness above.

"Have you ever been to Earth?" she asked Stasya.

"Yes. A long time ago." Stasya rose abruptly and stepped toward the open door.

"Where are you going?"

"I'll be back." That was all the answer Mitsuko was going to get, and she had better get used to it. Stasya closed the door behind her, leaving Mitsuko and her guard on the balcony.

A young maid looked up from cleaning up the remains of Mitsuko's toilette. "Can I help you, ma'am?" she asked.

"Yes, you can. Margo, was it?"

"Yes, ma'am."

Stasya closed the distance between them until she was close enough to make Margo nervous. "I need a favor, Margo. I need a set of grays. Women's large."

Margo's eyebrows shot up as she realized they were for Stasya. "Grays, ma'am?"

Stasya nodded, a smile both sly and bashful taking over her face. Far better for Margo to think she and Mitsuko played kinky games than for her to guess the truth. "Please, don't ask why. I just…can you bring me some? Without…making a fuss about it?"

Margo opened her mouth, then shrugged. "Yes, ma'am, of course. But…" Stasya was already reaching into her pocket for her handheld. She accessed Elissa Nakamura's credit account, punched in a debit amount, then held it out to Margo for inspection. "The cost of materials, plus a gratuity for your discreet assistance."

Margo smiled and nodded, and held out her hand so Stasya could scan the debit to her I.D. "Thank you, ma'am."

"No, thank you, Margo. You can just tuck them away in Ms. Jennings-Villega's closet, perhaps? Where they're not likely to…get in anyone's way."

Margo grinned. "Yes, ma'am."

The door to the balcony opened. "Elissa? Are you…Oh. There you are. Are you ready to go?"

Stasya's smile was firmly in place when she turned back around, the handheld snug in her pocket. "Of course, love."

Mitsuko's High Street mask could not hide the glimmer of curiosity in her eyes. "Let's go, then."

Stasya almost made it through lunch before she had to excuse herself to the ladies' room just to get a moment alone. She locked herself in a stall and opened her small handbag to remove a carefully pilfered pastry. Mitsuko and her friends might be able to nibble at their food after a morning of drug-induced hyperactivity, but Stasya needed nourishment. She chewed the roll with her eyes closed in pathetic pleasure.

The door creaked open and a woman's shoes clicked on the tile floor. Stasya waited for her to take the other stall, but instead, the footsteps kept coming until they paused in front of Stasya. "You're dripping crumbs," Mitsuko noted.

Stasya glanced down and saw the treacherous bread crumbs littering the floor between her feet. "Sorry. I'm starving."

"I offered you a dose, but you had to play big-bad-assassin-staying-on-her-toes, remember? Let me in."

"What? No." Stasya frowned at the door, as if Mitsuko could see her expression through it.

Mitsuko rapped impatiently on the door. "Come on, nobody will come in until we leave. They think we're in here making out."

"Yeah, speaking of that." Stasya unlocked the door and swung it open, leaving Mitsuko to jump aside before it smacked her. "Could they stare a little more? I feel like a zoo exhibit."

Mitsuko smirked. "Oh, it's worse than that. Welcome to the world of corporate celebrity. We'll be the talk of the colony by tonight. I've never done this before, you know. Everyone is thrilled for me—my first foray into extramarital affairs, and I get the exotic new girl." Her mouth twitched in genuine mirth. "Oh, wait until Daddy sees the pics…He'll have a coronary."

Stasya blinked. She had known their companions were taking pictures—too many telltale glints from their sunglasses—but she hadn't realized the photos would be making quite so many rounds. "But we haven't…I mean, we've just held hands—"

"And looked," Mitsuko said, giving her an exaggerated leer. "Don't forget the looks."

"Right, the looks. So all that 'calculated discretion' we talked about?"

"But we're doing wonderfully. Just enough to keep the girls winking and nudging, without giving Napoleon grounds for legal action." Mitsuko raised an eyebrow. "Besides, it's not the photos, it's the gossip that goes with them. Making an otherwise innocent picture juicier with a personal story that may or may not be entirely true is the real fun."

"Corporate spouses have odd ideas of fun. Is this what we're doing, all afternoon? Shopping and gossiping and ordering expensive meals that we don't actually eat?"

Mitsuko nodded. "All in the name of good business. Try not to lose your mind where people can see, darling." She took Stasya's hand, brought it up to her mouth and licked a fingertip. "Mm. Strawberry." The mischievous spark in her eyes turned warmer. "Does your mouth taste like that?"

Stasya lowered her head, bringing her lips to within centimeters of Mitsuko's. She hovered there, waiting, until Mitsuko pouted and opened her eyes. Then she grinned. "Get your own," she whispered.

Mitsuko smacked her on the arm but allowed Stasya to back her out of the stall.

"I didn't hear Frances come in." Stasya asked, glancing around suspiciously. "What happened to her unhealthy obsession with not letting you go to the can alone?"

"Astoundingly enough, she volunteered to wait outside. Even she has her limits." Smiling, Mitsuko paused at the mirror and mussed her hair, just a little.

◆◆◆

"I'm beginning to see why you think death is the better option." Stasya slumped against the cushions, toeing off her shoes. It was her third night in High Street, and the strain was beginning to take its toll. She was tired and ravenously hungry; and dealing with the members of Mitsuko's social circle was pushing her to the edge of her sanity.

"So hurry up and kill me if you're so miserable," Mitsuko snapped. "The sooner you finish the job, the sooner you can be on your way." She rose and went into her bedroom, stripping off clothes as she went.

Stasya almost let it go, but her nerves were frayed and her irritation got the better of her. She followed Mitsuko into the bathroom. "I could have been finished with this three nights ago, if you hadn't decided you needed to dictate the circumstances of your death."

Mitsuko turned on the water and raised her voice to be heard over the noise. "So I didn't want to die in a public bathroom to be stared at by pompous, gossiping idiots. What's wrong with that?"

"You're going to be dead. What difference does it make?"

Mitsuko opened her mouth and closed it, then appeared to focus her attention entirely on whether the water was the right temperature. She decided it was, for she stepped into the shower and pointedly closed the screen in Stasya's face.

Stasya jerked it right back open. "I asked you a—" Her anger died at the look on Mitsuko's face. She wasn't crying; Mitsuko wasn't the sort to cry. But she looked…hurt.

Lost.

Stasya lowered her head. "Sorry."

Mitusko turned to look at her. Water sheeted over her face and ran down her body in rivulets; body paint pooled in glittery swirls around the drain. "What are you going to do with me?"

"What do you mean?"

"After…after it's done. Are you…are you going to leave me where I fall, or…or stuff me down the incinerator chute, or …?"

Stasya frowned. "I hadn't thought about it yet." It was true. She'd been concentrating on her own escape, gathering materials from people like Margo, making arrangements with Rupi and a few trusted contacts Rupi didn't know about, just in case. And, though Stasya hated to admit it to herself, she didn't like to think of Mitsuko as a corpse. Her conscience, which Stasya thought had gone the way of her training bra, must have decided to make a surprise visit. "It's supposed to be a crime of passion, right? Why think ahead?"

Mitsuko stared at her, then turned her face back toward the spray. "I'll be out in a minute."

"Yeah." Stasya closed the shower screen, her mouth still wrenching downward. She didn't move, but stood in front of the shower, watching the movements of Mitsuko's blurred silhouette.

"Why didn't you kill me the first night? Why did you even bother with what I wanted?"

Stasya shook her head, a movement too subtle for Mitsuko to see through the screen, if she was even looking.

The shower shut off and the screen slid open. Mitsuko regarded her, blinking water out of her eyes. "I didn't hear you."

The water beaded on Mitsuko's eyelashes, held Stasya rapt and motionless for a few heartbeats. Her gaze traveled down Mitsuko's body, and she knew that if she pulled that body against her, it would soak her clothes and smear her body paint and it would be warm and welcoming and she could lose herself in it. She tried to imagine that same body, draining of blood, cooling on the carpet beside the window as the lights of High Street twinkled and danced on her skin.

"I don't know," she finally said, her voice low and flat. She took the towel from its hook and tossed it at Mitsuko, then strode out of the steamy bathroom and into the bedroom. For the first time since arriving at the Villega suite, she reached for the button to ring a maid. She needed a drink.

A wet hand stopped her. "Don't. I don't want anyone here now."

Stasya turned to find Mitsuko wrapped in the towel, but still dripping onto the carpet. With her hair plastered to her head and shoulders, her body contracting a little from cold, she looked small, and afraid. "What's wrong?" Stasya asked. Mitsuko took a breath. "Do it, Elissa. Do it now."

"Mitsuko, there's no—"

"Just do it, please, I can't stand waiting anymore." Mitsuko put her hands over her face, then clenched them into fists. "I want it over. I don't want to think about it anymore. Please."

Stasya moved forward and took Mitsuko's wrists, tugging until she brought them away from her face. "You don't have to think about it at all," she murmured. "I'm taking care of everything."

Mitsuko's eyes were wide, her face pale. "Please, do it now," she whispered.

Stasya stared at her. "I can't."

"Why not?" Mitsuko's face crinkled as if she might cry after all. Stasya gave in to a need to pull her close, to comfort her, anything to keep the last of her dignity intact. Silent and trembling, Mitsuko clung to her. One part of Stasya's mind disappeared into Mitsuko's closeness and the irresistible desires that flared wherever she made contact with warm, naked skin. The other part was still trying to think of an answer to Mitsuko's question. Yes, there were a few arrangements of her escape that would go smoother if she waited, a few details that would make Napoleon's denials more convincing, but they were extras, icing on the cake. When it came down to it, she could kill Mitsuko anytime.

Anytime.

Mistuko's weight shifted, and Stasya felt her move. She jerked before her mind registered it was Mitsuko's fingers on her cheek, urging her to turn her face and look down. She did.

Mitsuko searched her eyes, a strange half-smile on her lips. "You like?"

Stasya let her gaze wander again over the gold and porcelain perfection of Mitsuko's body. She sighed. "Yes."

The smile blossomed into fullness. "I hoped you would." She moved her hand up into Stasya's hair, combing through it with short, gentle strokes. "Come to bed with me."

Stasya almost said no. She had suggested the notion of a lovers' quarrel to her to avoid a painful mess, and to make her own planning easier. She hadn't meant for it to be real.

Of course, 'real' could mean many things, on the edge of death.

Feeling light kisses on her throat, Stasya lifted her hands to touch Mitsuko's face, shaking with the stubborn urge to put a stop to it. Then she closed her eyes and exhaled and pushed Mitusko the few steps to the bed. Mitsuko sat on the edge and Stasya leaned down to her. "Don't scream," she growled into one small ear. "I don't want your guards rushing in here."

Mitsuko bit her lip and nodded obeisance. Twining her arms around Stasya's neck like a warm, silky vine, she lay back and drew Stasya down with her.

Mitsuko amazed Stasya. For a woman who seemed to know so well what she wanted, and to know so well how to get it, Mitsuko became a creature of astounding innocence once she placed herself in Stasya's hands. The artifice, the sophistication, the seduction, all fell away and she responded to Stasya's touch with such honest desire that Stasya could not help but give her anything she wanted. With her body and her voice and her eyes Mitsuko made wishes, and Stasya did her best to grant them.

Stasya made no wishes of her own; there was no point. Mitsuko was going to die. It wasn't real.

◆◆◆

Rupi's eyes were so wide they nearly filled the screen of Stasya's handheld. "You haven't done it yet? I thought you were calling me from a swanky resort to tell me to hurry up with the rest of the payment. And you say you haven't even done it yet? What's going on, babe? You run into trouble?"

Stasya's hand curled over her mouth for a second before she answered. She knew better than to assuage him by telling him Napoleon had approved the delay. Rupi tended to frown on side deals. "No. No trouble. Just a change of plans."

Rupi pursed his lips, skeptical. "Changing plans isn't usually your style."

"I know. This job's turned out a little different than I expected."

"Obviously. So when will I hear good news from you?"

"Tonight. Late."

Rupi nodded. "All right. Talk to you then."

Stasya cut the connection but didn't move. Even out on the balcony, she suddenly felt claustrophobic, the towers of High Street too close, too high around her.

"Everything okay?" Mitsuko's sleepy voice broke the relative silence. She leaned against the doorframe, her hair mussed, clad only in a light blanket she held loosely around her with one hand.

Stasya glanced at her, then concentrated on removing her earpiece and laying her handheld carefully on the table. "Yes. Fine."

Mitsuko stepped onto the balcony, pulling the door closed behind her. She walked around the table to the low wall, put her hands on the rail, and looked down. "I haven't been up this early in years. It's so quiet."

"Mm."

She stayed at the wall a moment longer, then turned and put her back to it. "Will it be hard for you to escape?"

Stasya shook her head. "I've planned it pretty well. Don't worry about it."

Mitsuko smiled. "I do worry about it. Is that strange? I worry about things that will happen after I'm gone, like they'll matter to me. Like how I didn't want to die in the bathroom, where people would gawk at me. I didn't want to become one more spectacle to entertain the High Street vultures for a few hours before something else got their attention."

"That's not strange."

"But I worry about Napoleon, too, and whether he'll pull

himself out of this mess he's in."

Stasya snorted. "Why do you worry about him? He's paying me to kill you, remember?"

"I don't know. Maybe because I know I'm doing someone some good, for the first time in my life, and I don't want it to be for nothing."

"That's really pathetic."

Mitsuko laughed. "It is, isn't it? I don't always feel that way. Just lately."

"Impending death will do that to you."

Mitsuko turned back around to look over the wall again. "You could it right now. You could throw me over the side."

"You could do that yourself."

Mitsuko didn't reply, and didn't move. Stasya got up from her chair and crossed to stand behind her. She slid one arm around Mitsuko's waist and put one hand over her throat, tilting her head back. Mitsuko gasped, but didn't struggle.

"Do you want me to do it now?" Stasya hissed in her ear.

She felt Mitsuko swallow, felt the pulse in her neck speed up. "Please, Elissa…"

"Please, what?"

Mitsuko only whimpered in response. Stasya whirled her around, shoving her roughly against the low wall so that her back arced slightly over the handrail. Her brown eyes were wide and she gripped Stasya's forearms tightly enough to bruise. The blanket slid to the ground at Mitsuko's feet.

"Please, what?" Stasya asked. "Are you finally afraid of me?"

Mitsuko turned her head to look down, and squeezed her eyes shut. Stasya pushed her harder against the rail, then leaned down and kissed her neck, just beneath her jaw. Mitsuko gasped again, softer this time.

"You want to know what I'm going to do when you're dead? I'm going to leave the colonies. I'm taking your husband's money and I'm going to Earth. I'm going to walk on the beach barefoot and feel the salt water wash over my feet." She kissed Mitsuko again, lower on her throat, then moved down to suckle a small, brown nipple. Stasya felt her arm released, felt clutching fingers in her hair. The sound that came from Mitsuko's throat was not fear.

"What do you want from me?" Stasya slid her hand down to the curls between Mitsuko's legs and into the wetness she found there, eliciting a moan and a tug on her hair. Receiving no further answer to her question, she smirked and pressed her fingers into Mitsuko's body. "They're watching us," Stasya murmured. "In the buildings across from us, on the street below us. Everyone can see you. How will you face them tonight, knowing they all saw me do this to you?"

Keeping one hand at the back of Stasya's neck, Mitsuko relaxed her body and arched over the wall, her hair hanging down like a flag. Stasya plunged her fingers in and out of Mitsuko's slick warmth, sucking hard on her breasts, until she felt a familiar tightening in Mitsuko's stomach muscles, heard her moan even as she shivered in aching restraint. Stasya lifted her head. "You're too quiet."

Mitsuko cried out, louder than Stasya expected, and it made her smile. The residents of High Street would be waking up early this morning.

As the echoes faded, Stasya pulled Mitsuko upright, but Mitsuko wasn't ready to do any more than hang bonelessly in her arms. Stasya leaned down to pick up the blanket and wrapped it around Mitsuko, just enough for a semblance of modesty. "Tell the guards we're fine."

"What?"

As if on cue, the balcony door burst open and two suited men appeared. "Ma'am?" the first one barked, his eyes sweeping the scene.

Mitsuko smiled over Stasya's shoulder. "We're fine, Hammond," she said, a hint of a giggle in her tone. "Leave us alone."

Lowering his eyes, Hammond cleared his throat and gestured to the other guard to beat it. When the door closed again, Mitsuko lay her head back down.

"What do you want from me?" Stasya asked again. This time, though, the edge in her voice demanded an answer. "I need to know. Now."

"I don't want—" Mitsuko stopped as if frightened by her own admission. She drew in a shuddering breath, "I don't want to die."

"That's what I thought," Stasya whispered.

For a long time, neither of them moved.

"Mitsuko, do you trust me?"

"Yes." She lifted her head and looked into Stasya's eyes. "I trust you."

Holding that gaze, Stasya stopped breathing. She knew well enough what it felt like to hold a life quivering in her hands. But it had been a long time since she'd held a life she didn't want to let go of. A life she wanted to keep safe.

"I trust you," Mitsuko said again, but she smacked lightly at Stasya's shoulder. "Except you're a liar. Nobody is awake yet, to have been watching."

Stasya smirked. "They're awake now. Besides, what makes you think I meant your friends? The labor district has been awake for hours."

"But you said 'face them tonight'..."

"Does the food serve itself?"

Mitsuko blushed pink and lowered her eyes. "I…forget."

"Everyone does. Wearing gray makes you invisible. It's how I've stayed alive for so long." Thinking about grays made Stasya pause and look thoughtfully at Mitsuko.

"What?"

"Nothing. But I just realized that if this is going to work, I have a lot more work to do." She disengaged from Mitsuko's arms.

"Wait."

Stasya stopped. "What?"

"I've wanted to ask…" A teasing sparkle came into Mitsuko's eyes, but it wasn't enough to hide her uncertainty from Stasya. "What's your real name?"

Yesterday, Mitsuko would have known better than to ask that question. Today, everything was different. Still, Stasya hesitated, hating the moment of no return even as she surrendered to its inevitability. "Elissa is my real name."

Mitsuko arched an eyebrow and Stasya sighed. "I've been Anastasya Jonak for longer than I was Elissa Nakamura. Stasya."

"Stasya. Okay. Where are you from?"

"Jin Myung." Stasya paused, entertaining the crazy notion that Mitsuko's curiosity would be satisfied with that.

Of course, it was not. Mitsuko was nothing if not perceptive. "Why did you leave?"

Stasya licked her lips and shifted from foot to foot, hating this story. "Remember how I said I knew all about divorce lawyers?"

"I remember," Mitsuko said softly. "Was it bad?"

"Bad. Yes, it was bad. One of the most spectacular custody fights you've ever seen. They hated each other and I hated both of them. By the time the dust settled, my choices were living in working class squalor in the Greenhouse Zone with my mother or living…well, your life."

Mitsuko made a sound of sympathy.

"I put up with the lawyers and the tug-of-war for just over two years, and then…" She chuckled, a little harshly. "I got out. For good."

"You ran away?"

"No. I died." She paused again, this time to see the expression on Mitsuko's face. "Our housekeeper's daughter died of a drug overdose. High Street indulges in the best imports and Enforcement looks the other way, but in the labor district, drugs are bad news. They get cheap, dangerous stuff and the laws are draconian. If word had gotten out of how the girl died, the mother could have been sent to jail for it. So, we came to an arrangement where we each got what we needed. I've been Stasya ever since."

"Why did you become a killer?"

"Because the money's good. Like I said, the busboy isn't as happy as you think he is." Stasya shrugged. "I may also have had some unresolved anger issues to work through."

Mitsuko was silent for a moment, her expression far away. Stasya bit back the urge to ask her what she was thinking. "Mitsuko, if this going to work, I'm going to need you to do exactly as I say, no questions asked."

Mitsuko's nodded. "I will."

"It won't be easy."

She smiled, and for the first time since Stasya had met her she looked genuinely happy. "Don't worry about me. I'm ready."

◆◆◆

That evening, Mitsuko was sharper than usual with her maids. It might have been to hide nervousness—or embarrassment, if she had taken Stasya's teasing to heart that morning—but Mitsuko was clever enough she might have been doing it to add layers to their charade. Whatever the source, Stasya made a show of pretending not to notice, and even shared a quick look of commiseration with Margo when Mitsuko's back was turned.

Mitsuko did look stunning when the maids were finished. She wore red, deep and vibrant against her gold-toned skin. She left her hair long and loose, sprayed with a light layer of crimson glitter. Her eyes were painted large and smoky, and looking at her, Stasya caught herself wondering how she could possibly have ever seen Mitsuko as just another pretty target.

Stasya's handheld beeped with an incoming call and she ducked out onto the balcony to take it, curving the thin wire of a subvocal pickup around her throat for privacy.

"What the hell are you doing, babe?"

"And a very good evening to you, too, Rupi. I take it you have a question about my last message."

"Damned right I do. What do you need with another blank service I.D.? Don't tell me yours has been blown; I won't buy it."

"Rupi, do you trust me?"

"Not in a million years, babe; you know that."

"Yeah, I know that. Okay, then, how about 'change of plans'?"

"You've used that one already."

"That's all you're getting."

"It's not enough."

Stasya's mouth hardened. "The target dies tonight. That's all you need to know, and all the client needs to know."

Rupi sighed. "Fine. I don't guess you've ever let me down before."

"Thanks for the effusive praise," Stasya muttered. "So, will I have a delivery at the drop or not?"

"Yeah, yeah, fine."

"A *clean* I.D., Rupi."

"Hey, I'm an honest businessman, babe."

Stasya gave him a dubious frown and broke the connection. She stuffed her handheld back into her evening bag and slung it around her wrist. The balcony door opened and Stasya's favorite guard looked out. "Ms. Nakamura?" Frances intoned stiffly. "Ms. Jennings-Villega is ready to go."

"I imagine so," Stasya said. Frances held the door for her as she stepped past but offered her nothing else in the way of courtesy.

Mitsuko stood just behind the open door, arms crossed

and a scowl on her face. "Who was that?"

Stasya blinked. "No one…"

"Don't tell me 'no one.' You've been getting mysterious little calls for two days now. I think you're hiding something from me, Elissa, and I don't like it at all."

"What the hell are you talking about?" Stasya asked.

"You just waltz into High Street and into my life and I don't know who you left behind on New Ginza, or Jin Myung, or wherever else you've lived—"

Stasya gave her a bemused laugh. "You're imagining things, love." Stasya stepped forward and attempted to put her arms around Mitsuko, who shoved her away with surprising strength.

"No, leave me alone. Let's just go. We'll be late." Mitsuko flounced off, leaving Stasya to follow behind her. Frances gave Stasya a long look before she took her post beside Mitsuko.

Napoleon joined them at the elevator. During her stay, Stasya had made it a point not to meet his eyes when they were together—the man could hide nothing—but Mitsuko's silence was so stiff that Stasya made small talk with him just to break it. The instant the doors opened, though, Mitsuko was all smiles, melting into her husband's side when he put his arm around her, laughing and holding Stasya's hand as she exchanged greetings and air kisses with the luminaries of her social circle. Business as usual.

Stasya sat at Mitusko's side for the meal, but deliberately chatted with her other neighbor rather than Mitsuko. Playing her part, waiting for her cue.

Frances seemed to be keeping a closer eye than usual on Stasya tonight. She wondered if their hallway tiff had been a little too convincing. Otherwise, dinner went smoothly despite the noticeable chill from Mitsuko. Even one of the other guests commented on it, asking Mitsuko if she were feeling all right.

"She's fine," Stasya snapped, overhearing. "She's just cranky because she missed her afternoon fix."

Mitsuko spoke without looking at her. "He wasn't talking to you, love."

Stasya saw the perfectly composed smile on Mitsuko's face, and nearly grinned herself. Mitsuko might have lived a sheltered High Street life, but it certainly had made her a great actress.

Mitsuko waited a beat, then turned around. "You know, this is getting a little tiresome."

"What is?" Stasya affected deliberate nonchalance.

"You. Over the past few days, you've taken this notion that I'm your full-time submissive or something. You tell me how to dress, what I can eat, what drugs I can take, what I can drink, how to act…It was a cute little game at first, but I'm over it now. You're not that good."

Stasya laughed nervously and glanced around at their dinner companions, all of whom appeared to be concentrating fiercely on their desserts. Stasya knew their ears were wide open, though, their peripheral vision straining for details. After this was over, they would gather in small groups and compare their patchy versions of what they had seen and heard. "Why, I don't know what you're talking about, love."

"And stop calling me that. It's demeaning."

"Demeaning?" Stasya let anger subsume her previous embarrassment. "What the hell are you talking about?"

"Oh, my," Napoleon broke in. He smiled broadly around the table, but his chuckle sounded forced. "I know there's nothing you ladies like better than a dramatic little scene, but the crème brulée is really too delicious to miss."

Soft, relieved laughter trickled around the table, and Mitsuko made a point of suddenly noticing the oblique attention of the other guests. Her face and body closed down beneath a suitably agreeable blush, and her voice lowered to a venomous murmur. "Maybe we should discuss this in private, after dinner."

"Maybe we should." Stasya picked up her coffee with a hand that visibly trembled.

They stayed through dinner only because it would have been terrible form to leave early. Though Mitsuko put her gracious smile back on, Stasya never ventured out from her morose annoyance, and no one tried to speak to her. As soon as they could, she and Mitsuko took their leave. Stasya felt the eyes of the other diners on her back as she followed a nearly stomping Mitsuko to the elevators. The guard assigned to escort them back to the suite had to jog to catch up.

"Excuse me."

Mitsuko scowled at her. "Something wrong, Frances?"

Frances's reply was a broad gesture of invitation to precede her to the lifts. Stasya touched Mitsuko lightly on the arm to nudge her forward. If there was anything wrong, privacy was the best circumstance.

Frances waved her hand in front of the I.D. scanner and requested their floor, seemingly oblivious to Mitsuko and Stasya's sullen silence.

When they reached Mitsuko's suite, Frances followed them in. As the door slid shut, she glanced toward it and said, "Lock." The door beeped in response.

Mitsuko's body tensed. "What's going on?"

Frances ignored her and turned to Stasya. With one hand she brushed back her uniform jacket to reveal a shoulder holster and a police-grade dart gun. "I brought you here to arrest you, Ms. Nakamura."

Mitsuko gasped, but Stasya laughed. "Arrest me? Are you insane? On what grounds?"

"On the grounds that you're supposed to have been dead for over ten years. Now, I don't know who you are or how you got Elissa Nakamura's I.D. implant, but one way or the other, you have some explaining to do. So if you'll just come along quietly, we can avoid embarrassing Ms. Jennings—"

"Dead?" Stasya had kept up the act through Frances's explanation, opening and closing her mouth as if she couldn't believe what she was hearing. "Dead? Excuse me, but I think I'm the expert on whether I'm dead or not. Why in the world would you think something so absurd?"

Frances hesitated just long enough to let Stasya know that she hadn't lost her touch. "Well, Ms. Nakamura, we checked up on you a little. Under orders," she clarified, seeing Stasya's ire rising again.

"Orders from whom?" Mitsuko demanded.

Frances tightened her lips. "Alexander Jennings."

Mitsuko mouth thinned. "Daddy."

Frances snorted. "Yeah, Daddy. He likes to know who his daughter is…associating with."

Mitsuko tilted her head and eyed Frances. "And how does Daddy find out who I am…associating with?"

A smirk crossed Frances's mouth. "Who doesn't know?"

"So you do report to Napoleon after all?"

"No, ma'am. It's not my job to report to your husband when you have an affair. It is my job to report it to your father."

Mitsuko was angry, now, and Stasya silently cheered her on. She took a step toward Frances, studying her face. "And your pleasure, too, if I'm any judge."

Frances shrugged.

"You bitch." Stasya saw Mitsuko move, but Frances was too slow. Before she could collect herself to dodge or block, Mitsuko had landed a resounding slap across her face. "And to think I stood up for you when you nearly let the last assassin get through."

Frances dropped back a step, one hand on her cheek. With the other she calmly reached under her jacket for her tranq gun. She leveled it at Mitsuko.

"I think you might be getting a little too excited, ma'am,"

Frances said, dryly.

    Stasya tugged Mitsuko behind her and slammed her foot into Frances's hand. With a spitting sound and a plink, a dart fired into the ceiling. Frances pulled the gun back up but Stasya was on her. She grabbed Frances's wrist, driving her fingers into the soft spots until Frances's fingers released. The gun fell to the floor and Mitsuko darted forward to scoop it up and away.

    Frances swung at Stasya with her free hand. Exploiting Frances's sudden nearness, Stasya dragged her forward then came up from behind and locked her arm around Frances' throat.

    Frances was no fool; she knew she had only a few seconds. With a raspy curse, she fought the best she could from her pinioned position, thrashing her body and clawing at Stasya's forearm. But Stasya didn't give her time to get her feet beneath her for a real fight. When she felt Frances's body begin to slump into unconsciousness, she dug her fingers into Frances' hair and jerked hard. A mighty wrench, a sickening crack, and Frances sagged in her arms. Stasya slowly let her down.

    Mitsuko stood motionless, pale and staring, holding Frances' gun. "Is she dead? Just like that?"

    "Just like that. We're doing this now," Stasya warned. This was the test. If Mitsuko held together over the next few minutes, they would be fine. If she didn't...well, then, Mitsuko wasn't the woman Stasya had thought she was.

    Mitsuko blinked and nodded. "What do you need?"

    Stasya let a corner of her mouth crook upward and held her hand out for the gun. Mitsuko passed it over as if it had dirtied her fingers.

    "Ring for liqueur," Stasya said. "But don't let the maid in; I'll accept the tray." Looking around, she found what she needed, a demi-lune table against the wall. She dragged it over, climbed onto it, and reached up to pull the dart from the ceiling. She loaded it back into the gun, and tucked the gun into the top of her stocking so she would remember to properly dispose of it.

When that was done, Stasya sent Mitsuko into the large closet with directions for locating the tote bag containing the grays Margo had delivered the day before. The door chimed to announced the maid's arrival with the tray before Mitsuko came back.

Stasya ruffled her hair and slid the strap down on her dress, exposing a breast, as she stepped to the door's manual control. She let it open halfway before she hit the halt button, so her body blocked the maid's already limited vision into the room. "I'll take it," she said, giving the maid a breathless smile. The maid blushed and handed the tray over, retreating as quickly as she could.

Mitsuko watched impassively as Stasya poured two glasses of cordial and gave one to her. "Drink."

They both sipped from their glasses. Stasya set hers back on the tray after one swallow, but Mitsuko took one more before she did the same. "Why did we do that?"

"Verisimilitude. Follow me."

Stasya led Mitsuko to her dressing table, where she tied Mitsuko's hair back with a scarf at the nape of her neck. Reaching into one of the small drawers, she pulled out a tiny pair of scissors the maids used to snip loose threads on Mitsuko's clothing. Stasya used them to saw at Mitsuko's hair.

Seeing in the mirror what Stasya was doing, Mitsuko bit her lip, but said nothing as she watched Stasya work. At last Stasya held a hank of silky black hair, still glittering red, tied with the scarf. She put the hair into a plastic bag that went into the tote bag with the grays. Mitsuko put her hand to her raggedly cut hair, touching it as if she couldn't believe it was gone.

Moving quickly from one task to the next, Stasya went back out into the sitting room, where Frances still sprawled indelicately across the cushions. Grasping the slender neck of the liqueur decanter, she brought it crashing down against the edge of the table. The bulbous bottom sheared off and bounced across the carpet, flinging sticky red drops behind it. In her hand Stasya held the crystal neck, now bearing a wickedly lethal edge.

"Why did you do that?" Mitsuko asked, her voice small.

Stasya turned slowly. "I need something to kill you with, love. Something that will leave a lot of blood." She reached for Mitusko's hand and jerked her forward. "Now, hold still."

Mitsuko took a deep breath and closed her eyes.

❖❖❖

Stasya stood in line at the New Chueca airport, a dreadful place of battered institutional decor and terrible acoustics. She stepped up to the check-in and lifted her right hand.

The scanner beeped, and a pleasant female voice proclaimed, "Anastasya Jonak, service, confirmed for flight."

She smiled at the attendant and strode forward into the docking sleeve. After a few steps, she bent down to fix the strap on her shoe and listened. This was the last real hurdle. If word had gone out to look for a woman who had cut out her I.D. implant, they would be in trouble now,

Behind her, the scanner beeped again. "Cynthia Parisi, service, confirmed for flight."

"Wondered if it was going to read through those bandages," rumbled the attendant. "What did you do to your poor little hand?"

A tinkling giggle. "Maybe I punched my boyfriend. You better watch out."

The attendant laughed. "Have a good trip, Miss."

Stasya shook her head as she straightened, wondering how she could for a moment have doubted Mitsuko's abilities.

Quick, light footsteps caught up to Stasya. "I can't believe I have to go through life with a name like Cynthia."

"You don't like it?" Stasya asked.

"It's all right, I guess," said Mitsuko. "But I'm not really a Cynthia, am I?"

"You can be a dead Mitsuko or a Cynthia on her way to Earth. Take your pick."

"Suddenly I'm feeling more like a Cynthia."

Stasya ducked her head as they crossed the threshold onto the transport. The cabin was already crowded, and her stomach turned chilly with dread as she caught sight of the stasis-sleep rigs and their silver IV needles. No matter how often she traveled, she never felt comfortable being knocked out in a room full of strangers.

Mitsuko had been assigned a seat several aisles back, and by previous arrangement, they did not speak again. Stasya glanced back at her once, to see her already buckled in, sitting stiffly upright. She kept her head lowered, though, letting her short hair fall forward to shadow her eyes. Between Frances's clothes and the high-backed seat, she looked small and pale. It struck Stasya that Mitsuko had never mentioned having traveled inter-colony before.

Stasya turned back to face the front as the flight attendant approached with her cart full of disinfecting swabs and surgical tape. It was too late to comfort Mitsuko now. Besides, Mitsuko was tough; she'd already proven that. She'd be fine.

Closing her eyes, Stasya listened to the crew go through their preflight routine, felt the transport move into place for take-off. When the engines roared, she began to relax for the first time in days. She wondered if Napoleon had reported his wife missing yet; if the guards had entered the blood-spattered sitting room and found the chunk of crystal covered in Elissa's fingerprints. Perhaps they were even now beginning to track the trail of droplets down the hall to the service recess, where a tiny, calculated smear of Mitsuko's blood decorated the edge of the incinerator chute.

If Colony Enforcement processed the chute properly, they would find a few glittery strands of hair that had floated up and escaped the inferno, and perhaps even a scrap or two of Mitsuko's bloody dress. Maybe tomorrow, but probably not for two more days, they would be able to sift through the cooling ashes from the incinerator. Someone would use tweezers to pull out the indestructible I.D. implant that declared the charred, disintegrated bones to be those of Mitsuko Jennings-Villega.

The stories would start to come out, from the servants, the guards, the other denizens of Zone Six East. They were fighting that night, seems they'd been playing some freaky little games that Mitsuko was getting tired of…Somebody said one of the servants had even procured a costume for them…Yes, that Nakamura woman had seemed a little off balance from the start. Dangerous combination, that.

The gossip would last for years, and improve with each telling.

Thanks to one of Stasya's talented and discreet friends, Frances had sent a text message to Alexander Jennings that she was going off-colony to pursue a lead on Mitsuko's mysterious new friend. Frances's I.D. implant was tucked safely into some tourist's luggage en route to Jin Myung. It would be a long time before she was missed.

Stasya smiled as she fell asleep. The job was done.

She awoke to the soft ding of the intercom, followed by the announcement that they were on approach to Earth. Fighting the annoying effects of the stasis sedative, she looked to the side, out a porthole, and saw it: a marbled blue ball suspended on black velvet.

It had been so long.

She turned in her seat and saw Mitsuko, still groggy from the flight. But she was gazing out the porthole, too, and in her eyes was a glow of childlike excitement. Stasya had not realized how badly she had wanted to see that look on Mitsuko's face. She resolved to bring it back as often as she could.

Cupcake

In the LAX port Stasya pulled Mitsuko over to the commuter flight schedule. The names of cities flashed by: Beijing, Buenos Aires, Paris, Nairobi, Moscow. "Where to?" Stasya asked.

Mitsuko looked at her and frowned. "What do you mean?"

"I mean, pick your new home."

"Me?" Mitsuko's mouth fell open and she looked at the schedule again. Uncertainty slowly became a broad smile. "Anywhere?"

Stasya leaned over and kissed her. "Anywhere."

Dead and the President

Tenea D. Johnson

DEAD AND THE PRESIDENT STROLLED DOWN THE LONG HALLWAY, flanked by Secret Service agents. None of the dark-suited men talked to the President, careful not to interrupt him before the State of the Union Address though each was wondering what he would say: if he would disclose what the latest environmental analysis said about the increasingly volatile world, if Northern Florida would soon join the rest of the panhandle under the sea and into memory, if he would discuss the restricted zones or the rumors of surgical bombing in South Carolina. It wouldn't have mattered if they asked. Inside the President, Dead could only hear the President's breathing and he could only hear hers. Focused on their separate missions, they did not think of each other or the others around them.

They were there now, standing in the shadows that sidled the bright blue stage, the White House insignia glowing in the lights. The press was corralled around the room—out of the way of the live holocam's beam splitter and mirrors, set to send Wesley's speech into every vid-equipped home and town square across the country. The cams whirred, awaiting President Burke's entrance. The Press Secretary called for quiet. Slowly the clamoring tide of questions ebbed.

Many articles had been written about Burke's gun collection. The weapons were hard to miss; they served as the background to every Presidential address, encased in a long plexiglass display behind his desk in the Oval Office. But tonight there was no flintlock rifle passed down hand to hand from Andrew Burke, a butcher of Seminoles, no cannon gun, no Rueger rumored to be fresh from the Fourth Reich, not even any Army prototypes named in strange binary codes. Tonight President Burke had only the antique 9mm holstered under his armpit—the one everyone had forgotten about because it'd become too common, too much of a gimmick to moor his words of self-reliance to their hearts.

Amid a smattering of applause, the President walked out to the podium. Dead let her prepared words slip away, released the morsel of relaxation she'd saved for this moment. Silence filled the room. Filled Wesley Burke. Filled the holocams.

Dead said with the President's voice:

"Thank you for coming. Welcome to the new day—"

She had just enough attention left to feel the cold metal press against his temple, feel the trigger jump from his finger. Hear the sharp intake of breath as the world stood still.

◆◆◆

Dead split. In her panic she bolted forward, and directly into the path of the holocam and its beam splitter. She was dispersed into pieces, and then into people—those in the room, and through the cam, those in the audience. Each bit of her shooting into unknowns.

◆◆◆

Mama Myrtha named me with protection in mind: nobody fucks with a girl dubbed Dead. And a girl, a Black girl, and an infinite Antibody besides, needs more protection than most. Especially in the Basin.

In the two years after Mama Myrtha had passed, I'd stayed clear of the Internal Processing Department, and their tagging and bagging. I'd seen folks trying to dig the tags out of the flesh without bleeding to death, but that was as close as I'd come. And anybody was apt to get bagged if the government wanted your business or your co-op or your whatever. Even the little little kids knew that; and I was already twelve years old. So tagging was just dark stains on the sidewalk to me. It went away with the rain.

So when the IPD transvan slid to a stop, blocking my path and with it, the sunlight, I breathed the next breath just like the one before it. Out of instinct, my second sight rose up, blurring the busy afternoon street into a field of bright life lights. I could have picked a light and phased into it, been staring out that person's eyes in less than a minute. Faster if I pushed my way in. But I couldn't chance that IPD would take my body when it dropped. If they did, I might not be able to come back to it. And if I did come back, IPD would find a new kind of Antibody, which would be me, and I would be fucked, even if they didn't fuck with me. So there I stood.

I couldn't fathom if the IPD beasts were bagging or tagging. The van just sat there, windows closed and engine idling. Vapors floated up from the hood and shimmered in the heat. Most days they were doing one or the other, sliding in quiet and striking where they liked. The Basin was full of Antibodies.

The air next to my ear split. A man standing behind me hit the ground, clutching his chest. Everyone else on the street froze, us we all waiting. An Olmejano causa vendor went down next, the side of her hand scraping the heating plate, flesh sizzling, reddening the intricate tattoos that ran up her arm, demarcating her profession. As she fell, a high-pitched beep bleated behind me. I didn't have to look to know it's a kid, the tag in his flesh bringing the beasts right to him.

A beast steps out of the other side of the trans, his IPD suit gleaming. The fabric shimmers when they step into the light. Nina told me once that it's like why they used to make cathedrals so tall: you'll be kind of in awe and then they can tag you quicker. I didn't even see the shot—just felt the tag burrowing into my back and left shoulder. The pain sent me down to one knee, my palm pressed against the street.

The beast walked past me and down to the alley where a little boy lay. He hoisted the kid over his shoulder and headed back to the van. Bagged.

A few breaths later, the transvan slid out and us we on the streets started moving again. Closer folks tended to the vendor and the man. I got up and started home. Then stopped on the corner and turned to the food hall instead. I had keep to my word to the kids. And the chip needed to come out; Nina would do the dig.

The tags ached. I pulled my collar down and looked at the one in my shoulder, an ugly black bump wiggling into my skin. It was smaller than the one that had come out of Nina, but bled just the same.

◆◆◆

By the time I entered the food hall, only the crown of the tag was visible—a black mark in the middle of a gray mound. I pulled the cloth back around my collar and focused on the hall. People packed the place, sitting and standing around long, low tables. It had been a shelter around the time the river ran over its banks and flooded out the old city. You could see the competing high water marks on the walls with just a strip of dirty white near the rafters, gradients of grime underneath. All of it a gray that repeated in the clothes of us we packed inside. For all the colors we were, we had the same uniform of ill-washed garments with the exception of the Olmejano in their bleached whites; some folks converted just to get clothes clean as a rich person's. People's voices echoed back and again with the sounds of utensils scraping against cheap plexi bowls, making the space seem even more crowded that it was. I saw Nina and the rest off in the corner, hawking the entrance. Twenty kids waiting on me, but they stayed still, kept their shitty looks for someone else.

"D—," Nina said, "You still?"

I nodded and kept walking toward the kitchen and serving window in the back of the room. It would be easier to get Nina aside after I fed the others. Was hunger that had brought me to the street in the middle of the day. These kids didn't get fed until I arrived. Before I'd started coming they just didn't get fed here. The food hall was supposed to be first come, first serve—but really the biggest ate before the fastest. A lot of kids fought on the street for their food. Some packed off to pleasure domes to earn their meals. I did what I could to stem that flow. 'Cause Dead don't' fear no death, but some things are worse than death. Still, most of the hall kids thought I was earning from one of the cooks for the food. The Olmejano thought I was a good luck charm. Maybe Nina and one or two others fathomed bits of the true.

When I got to the back counter, I saw the big man in charge of prep. I'd been phasing into Diso since long before Mama Myrtha passed, since him a boy and me a baby. He used to work the heating detail, but they'd moved him to the food hall. And Nina, knowing how warm our place always was, suggested that I make friends with the food line.

I'm a true-blooded infinite, but most us we Antibodies I'm only guessing at. Unless I'd been inside 'em, like the doublejack, Diso.

Sometimes the differences cloud even me and I do better than most folks. They've forgotten and can't fathom how we divide. But Mama Myrtha used to recite to me so forgetting I just can't do—Us we come straight from the genetic reparation generation. A lot of them would only fuck others who got reparations too. From there come your doublejacks, your squares, and your infinites. We still say doublejacks but only second-generation are true doubles; their children are squares, and then skip to infinite if your family always was Antibody going back three generations.

Diso was a double by way of his grandmothers so it was easy for him to get the job at the food hall; the government just concentrated on the side of him they could relate to, but still hadn't found a way to exploit the other. This because Diso was kind-hearted. He had a chest full of warm memories of his mama and dreams about the ocean so I didn't mind getting inside him. Plus Diso had a shit-shot reputation. None of the other cooks would front him about some extra food.

Diso lifted a net of chicken pieces out of a big metal vat and shook them out onto the counter. He worked alone, whistling to himself. I walked back to the kids and sat next to Nina. They hawked me till I told 'em, "chicken" then smiled to themselves. I put my head down on the table, getting ready to phase into Diso. The kids relaxed into waiting, figuring I'd done what needed to be done to get their meal and was catching the sleepsies, just as I always did far as they fathomed.

A lot of infinite Antibodies have sleepsies, an unfortunate side effect of being infinites.

Was a time, back when that big-brained man, Dr. Carter, first fixed the fetuses that all Antibodies were Black. At the core that was the reason: a "sorry we wronged you with slavery,"

Or truer still 'cause the government never paid and Dr. Carter got tired of waiting—

"They wronged us, but they ain't never gonna right it so here's something for the next ones."

Even before that, rich folks had been changing their babies for a decade. Somehow those first Europa doctors, and the Chinese and Indian ones too, thought they could control evolution once they stuck their foot in it. That the river would only run where they liked 'cause they funneled a stream. So now they were reduced to sending out IPD to bag and tag so they could try to track the changes and make themselves believe they were in control. Phasing has taught me nothing if not this: Folks will bend the world to their will, if only by what they acknowledge.

But control ain't nothing like you think it is.

With my eyes closed, my second sight was sharp and clear. The food hall crawled with light. The adults and kids in the room made an array of colors and sizes, pinpoints to spotlights. It took me years to get over the vertigo that accompanied second sight, but my control developed. Not only could I see each light in the room, but through the walls and beyond. Individual lights moved through the rest of the Basin, bunched in buildings and strung through the streets.

Even though I had always had second sight, I couldn't see the fence that surrounded the Basin until I was five, but gradually I learned to pull my perspective back so that the sawed-off mountains and abandoned mines beyond the blocks became visible. And on that day, I could see a band of light beyond the basin shining like a far off horizon.

Not yet knowing how close the horizon would soon come, I shrank my second sight back to the food hall and the meal at hand.

I concentrated on Diso's green flare of a light and pulled myself inside it. The big doublejack was a soft settle down to the bottom, so that I was like silt and he was the ocean floor. Phasing into some folks is walking across fire or shooting into a piece of wood, but Diso was gentle. So firstwise, I just floated through him and glided across his new memories and some of the old. Schools of his desires darted past in flashes of orange and yellow and a few old wizened satisfactions buoyed up and down in my wake. When I'd dissipated throughout him enough to rise up and look through his eyes, I saw the kids already lined up at the counter, bowls in their hands. Before Diso could wonder why they were there, I lured out an old song from his memory, one his mother used to sing that he could never remember the words to. Diso smiled, listening, and I walked him over to the counter. We picked up the kids' bowls. Nina handed him two, one of them mine. A few adults looked in Diso's direction, stared back down at their plates when I caught them with his sharp glare.

Humming, we filled the bowls with chicken and a thick yellow paste that Diso pulled from the industrial cooldown. When he brought the bowls back to the kids, he'd just finished the chorus for the fourth time. Inside, Diso was still and warm; I floated inside him swaying slightly in the current. The kids headed back to the table; I turned Diso in another direction and made him hawk the old man who was still staring. The coffin dodger hunched into the table, didn't look up. I packed Diso a meal and gathered me up and out, breaking the surface before he'd turned away from the counter.

Back at the table I lifted my head and smiled at him. He tilted his head at me, though he may not have known why. Some of the kids probably thought I was flirting; the rest were only interested in their bowls.

I knew one day I'd have to phase into Diso's boss or the one who told him which rules to follow or maybe even the boss of the man who made the rules, but back then I just showed up every other day to make sure Nina and the kids ate. Only later would I learn how many people it took to make real change.

After the meal, I stepped outside with Nina and started to tell her about the tag. I was already pointed at the direction of home and a sharp knife when a tall Yella from down the block started raising ruckus. I can't understand what he's saying cause he's from up around K block and I never did learn any patois past that what E block speaks.

As I squinted at him, trying to decipher the alarm in his voice, a screechy beeping washed down the block, coming from everywhere and going there too. Kids started breaking down the streets, knocking over carts and coffin dodgers. First I thought pleasure domers on a yes-girl run—trying to replace all the dead girls who'd said no. Then I saw the transvan. Nina, she squeezed my shoulder, then she was gone.

The sun had set, just a few slivers of light left. You would have thought I was invisible, but the beasts could see me. The

IPD man came right to me, barrel leveled at my chest. He was just about to pull the trigger when a shot rang out and a chip of the beast's IPD suit flew away. The beast pulled a handheld from inside his suit, aimed past me and shot. Then he smashed the butt of his weapon across my face and knocked me to the street. As he dragged me toward the van, I saw Nina's orange sneakers poking from behind a dumpster, cockeyed and at the wrong angle like she was snoring face up in the street. I stared at her shoes and put her name on that moment, making it the forever picture I've stored away.

I've learned to look at the hard things. 'Cause Mama Myrtha never told me, but I learned it just the same: Fear is worse than death.

◆◆◆

Three days later I lay strapped to a gurney, forgotten in a hallway in a too-bright building they tell you doesn't exist. The place where they take us to check what kind of new we are, if our magic is worth stealing for their own children. Far as they could tell, I was nothing special.

I lay there thinking of Nina's breath on my neck, whispering a story about the time before. Before Mama Myrtha had passed, before the Basin had flooded out, before we stayed in one place like we'd been born growing from the ground. While they poked, injected, hooked and unhooked me from quiet, colorful machines, and measured everything that came in and out of me, I lay there thinking of Nina and the promise we had made to one day change our world into someplace where we could rest when we wanted, eat our fill, and live out in the open.

I phased into an orderly as soon as we were alone and made him wheel me away from the loading dock of someone else's plans for me. But before he could move my body into the trunk of his car and smuggle me through the gates it broke on me that I could do more than survive.

No sudden moment of clarity like the sun breaking through that did it, but two bright tail lights coming straight at me: a truckload of food backing up to the dock. It was more food than a dozen Disos could provide, if I could get it back to the kids. It didn't take much to phase into the driver when he came to raise the rear gate of his haul. Run down as he was, he may not even have noticed me there, 'cause he conked out as soon as I came in and moving his body was like moving lead. The orderly never even looked back, just lined my body up with the other goods and gurneys and stepped out the exit. I walked the driver over to me, unstrapped my body and we were back out the gates just as the dockworkers walked out to unload the haul.

All my life, I'd only been inside the Basin and inside people who were in the Basin. The men and women who skittered around the edges of our zone fixing fences and delivering heating oil never much interested me, as small as that sounds. Even Mama Myrtha with her pictures from outside the fence and stories of the old Tennessee had lost the taste for freedom and so had taught me how to stay invisible, to stay strong, but always to stay, never to be more than I had always been. So I thought I could steal a truckload of food from the government and drive it back home with a little help from the truck's GPS. I thought that they only tracked us. But they track everything. Even before I saw the flashing strobes of the police trans in the rearview mirror, I began to reconsider my plan but by then it was too late.

After the driver had been taken into custody and the food turned back toward its origin, I rode inside an Officer Dimatulac, my body in the trunk of his police trans, gliding across the tracks that circled the Basin, climbing ever higher until we broke over lip of the hole I'd been born in.

◆◆◆

Topside staggered me. I have only traveled to a few places as jarring—and they were all inside people who inhabit the dark alleyways of the world. Orderly duocrete buildings lined the street, the only interruption a sculpted tree or tidy bush. The air didn't taste like fumes or even algae. To combat the look of peeling paint they seemed to have done away with it. All the personal trans shone steely silver in the sun. Dogs—which up to then I had only seen holos of—walked the streets with their owners. Us we weren't allowed pets and the few animals you saw in the Basin were on your plate or scurried past 'cause they were too hard to kill or trap. Must be that IPD had enough work cataloguing the effects of the Burn and Crumble on humans. And out here they didn't call it the Burn and Crumble, but "current environmental challenges" and "the adapting ecosystem."

Topside and the Basin only shared one thing: the omnipresence of holoposters. President Burke's image speckled the landscape, his stance holoed so that when people passed his presence leapt off of the paper, the antique steel of the gun in the holster glinting. The slogan, "We take care of ourselves," floated above Burke's head. Topside, his expression looked reassuring, like maybe he would protect you, not protect others from you. Nina and I had once spent an entire afternoon ripping down Burke's visage and tearing it to shreds. We didn't notice until halfway through C block that he was impossible to destroy. Every piece of the poster contained the entire image so we'd only succeeded in making more of him.

Those first few miles into Topside were enticing.

In the posh parts of Topside where the buildings stretched high in the sky, the posters changed. Ads for biogen adaptations began to show up on buildings. This more than all the other shocked. Us we'd been locked up and hunted for what might be in our genes, but out here they were still performing adaptations, selling them, coveting what they feared. It's as if folks thought it could still be controlled. The ads didn't acknowledge the unpredictability of what could happen a generation or two later when nature stepped back in to rebalance things. These people did not wonder what other Deads might be. I'd always wondered what else was possible if there was me.

I made Dimatulac deliver me to a crowded corner that reminded me of home. His grandmother lived in the flat above, so he considered it the safest place in the world and considering my knowledge of this world, I trusted his choice. He thought his lola hardly ventured to the basement so he left me there with food and supplies.

Of course no isolation lasts forever. When she finally did happen downstairs, I was in the bath. I caught her staring from the doorway, a look of stern disapproval settled on her otherwise soft features.

"Who are you?" She asked, her accent heavy. "I will call the police."

No one in the Basin's blocks sounded like her. It reminded me how far I'd come and how unprepared for the journey I was. Fascination kept me distracted and I lost my chance to direct the conversation.

"Nestor told me that I could stay here for a few days," I finally answered.

She looked at me steadily, one eyebrow slowly arching.

"Oh. Then I will not worry about it strange naked addict girl in my tub. Nestor, of course. I must have forgotten since I am so old and feeble." She turned and shuffled back upstairs, double-bolting the door behind her. Though I had to scramble to fathom what I would do now, I had to smile at her style.

She did call the police. Or one of them, at least. Not long after I heard Nestor upstairs. Their conversation permeated the aged wood of the basement door and floated down to me.

"There's a crash head in my basement," the old woman said.

"What? Lola, calm down, tell me again."

"I said there's a naked stinkwhore in my house says that you brought her here."

I imagine Nestor must have looked confused. I didn't know how much the folks I entered remembered or knew at the time. I'd reentered very few people and they let me back in so it had never concerned me. I'd been phasing since I was a baby. I took it for nature. Though I didn't think much about other folks at that age, if I had, I would've assumed that everyone could jump from body to body, that it was common to crawl inside other people and know their dreams, their memories, and what combination of magic caused this one's arm to raise or that one's fingers to twirl. When I found out otherwise, it didn't vex me much as shrink the world a bit.

But Lola didn't know that locking Dead up doesn't keep her from moving around. I closed my eyes and climbed into Nestor.

"She's a friend of mine."

"A friend?" her tone was sharp; this seemed to upset her more.

"A kid we picked up," I made Nestor say. "Her whole family was wiped out in that riot."

She didn't look impressed.

"Nestor, do I look like a shelter? Do you see soup and bums around here with my nice things? Do you?"

A thump from downstairs interrupted her. I knew what it was, but tried to ignore it and continue.

"And you never know there could be a re—"

"Shut up, Nestor. You hear that? I think that crash head fell."

Before we could answer she'd opened the basement door and was peering downstairs at where my body had landed when it slipped off the stairs. I'd fallen off the bottom step and onto the floor with my legs gathered beneath me. My head had collapsed into my chest, chin digging into my breastbone, arms akimbo.

"They giving rewards for how much crash she can ingest before she passes out? Jees! And just a girl that one."

"She's not toxxed." I said with Nestor's voice. "She's just tired."

"Tired of not being high maybe. That girl is barely alive, and you a policeman. Don't tell me she's not toxxed. Probably a little hustler. Is that what it is Nestor? You bring your peddyphile girlfriend to my home?"

"Lola, of course not. Like I told you she's—"

"She's toxxed. She's completely toxxed. She's toxxed all the time. I've been watching her. I know. She was high like that the day before yesterday, the day before that. And last week when you first brought her here. I walked right by her she didn't know. You think I don't know what goes on in my own house?! What you do in your marriage is between you and Marisol, but don't bring it here."

"She's not toxxed. She just needs some place to stay for a while and I thought this would be safe. That maybe she could help you around the house. Look, she's waking up now."

I zipped back into my body and moved around, trying to look lucid and pick myself up off the ground as gracefully as possible.

"It moves," she said, turning back to her grandson. She paused and asked, "What's wrong with you now?"

I looked up to the entrance where Nestor stood transfixed, staring at an open space off to his right. He blinked slowly, looked curiously at his grandmother.

"I, uh . . ." Nestor rubbed his forehead.

"You, 'uh' what?" his lola asked.

"What were we talking about?" he asked.

She narrowed her eyes. "The girl."

With my last bit of energy, I pulled myself toward the strong white beam that was Nestor's lola—Cecilia, I found out. The images inside her radiated stronger than any holo, bathing her in a wash of color—blues, orange, and red. One stood out among them. A bright swatch of memory with mounds of brown sunk into the blue in all directions. It took me a while to fathom this was an island surrounded by others; longer to know it was the archipelago that had become 'the Atlantisippines' always on the news. 2000 islands of the Philippines remained, another one swallowed regular as holocasts. Cecilia had seen them when there were still 2500 and cherished the memory. I tried to turn it to my advantage, but the place was the same as Lao Tse or Saturn to me. To double it, I could barely keep myself there; I'd never phased so many times so quickly. Before I could stop it my thought surfaced in her mind.

Floods, lady. I won't do you any harm. Just need a place for now. I lost all grip on her then and slid back to myself.

Nestor started down the steps, one hand on his weapon. All the cloudiness had cleared from his eyes. He came straight for me.

"I'll take her away, lola," Nestor said. "Don't worry."

Cecilia was staring down at the floor, one hand on her heart, the other braced against the door jamb. She shook her head gently and gave me a look that said she fathomed me all the way down.

"Oh." She straightened a bit. "Now you want to take her away. After all that fussing. No. She stays. You go." She saw him to the door then walked down the stairs and looked over my body, tilting my chin up and looking in to my eyes. "Quite a trick. Was what Nestor said about your family true?"

"They're gone, but not in a riot. Or at least not all of them that way. In different ways."

"Could any of them do what you can do?"

"No," I answered.

"Mine neither."

"What can you do?" I asked.

"I can tell when people are bullshitting," Cecelia said. "And I can tell when they stop. You hungry?"

"Yes, ma'am."

"Come upstairs, then. It's almost time for dinner."

◆◆◆

If you've ever suspected I can tell you for true: this ain't no democracy, bureaucracy rules. I've been inside 57 people on the way to figuring how to keep the hall children fed and more than that to straighten out heating oil in the winter. Getting the work done only took eight people, but getting it to stick, required the rest.

It took nearly six years to solve those two problems. I had my distractions. Without Cecilia's help I wouldn't have survived—even Topside.

My body battled through puberty to the leading edge of womanhood. Every time I came home to it I found something new—fuller, hairier, more sensitive than I had left it. But also taller, sleeker.

In those years, I learned how few people had any real power and how many others you had to go through just to find them. But on the way, I also found out how many restricted places there are in the country and got some idea of the number of ruined places in the world. They were laid out on a map inside a section chief's desk. Stray pen marks and worn spots had obscured a few of the sites, but the whole was intact. He had looked at the map years ago for a short term special assignment to have the borders of Pennsylvania tweaked to circumvent a sinkhole that had swallowed part of a county. When the project lost funding, he tucked the map into the back of his desk and tried very hard to forget it had ever existed. I did the opposite and worked to commit them all to memory: Red River Gorge, Snowshoe, Mojave 1, Gullah Gulch, Balboa Park Zygote, Sandhills Nebraska…

To find that you're not alone, not so unique might be bad news for some; but to find out your family is much larger, not dictated by the genetic code or natural disaster—it was almost as valuable as finding Cecelia and a safe place. When she became my name, Nestor took her ashes to her favorite island in all of the archipelago and I traveled to the capitol.

♦♦♦

I don't trust easy and I don't love light. People from hard places rarely do. Something good comes and you hide it, save it, and savor it every chance you get. But you make sure no one else is around before you do. So I tagged Xiomarys with my eyes the first time I saw her. She walked briskly across a crowded square, intent on some business that made her body lose all inefficiency, striking a grace that stopped every thought in my head. I'd just left the last link in the chain of command that handled food distribution to the projects on the Carolina coast, when she in her bright blue eyecatcha demanded my attention. Her hair hung a heavy black curtain that swayed with each step, revealing and hiding the golden skin and the elaborate Olmejano tattoos that ran up her neck.

I saw her again the next night, at the local grinder. One of the things worse than death is boredom and another is folks who can't dance. I try to avoid both. More than one person has taken themselves to be possessed not because their mind is strong and senses my presence but because of the way that I've made them move because a snippet of sound touched me from where I perched inside them. So on the few occasions when I could come home and stay a while, I found an underground grinder with live band or holo and got free. At the right grinder you could find anything you wanted. Music was mandatory, but the type comes any way you like, and with that there's smoke, drink, shoot, even crash if that's what you want. I liked the lighter spots for a dance, maybe a bowl, and back to a warm bed, usually my own.

Anxious after so much phasing, that night it felt good to be back with myself and surrounded by a rhythm other than foreign heartbeats and other folks' memories. The music grounded me, kept me from floating away. The grinder was only half-full. Of the folks standing around the bar I didn't see anyone special yet. It was the usual kind of crowd for women's night: folks from the fringes of the capital's culture mixed in with secret rebels who kept the city running by day, and maybe a few us we. A couple of men stood off to the side. I hoped they were together otherwise there were bound to cause trouble. I walked into the backroom. The music was better there—an old dragrocka and an instrumental from a new submersible soul group played one after the other so I stayed to dance. By the third song more women had arrived. I kept my eyes open while I moved, catching a gaze here or more there, but mostly just enjoying the view, nestled in my own head and its quieter thoughts— nothing more complicated than who lit me.

Xiomarys almost caught me ghosting—hazed from a smoke earlier and concentrating on nothing but the next move, I smelled something sweet and trying to place it, backed into her (later I wondered if she had put herself in my path). I turned to give my sorries and felt my eyes get bigger while my mouth kept moving. She'd seen the recognition-was always nothing or too much with me. I hadn't really learned how to be subtle in my own body so usually I stayed aloof. Women had accused me of barricading them off. It took me a long time to understand that most folks couldn't read you by the millimeter, couldn't know your thoughts at all unless you told them. Plus, I started to think right at that moment, could be those other women just didn't light me enough to read it on my face.

"Xiomarys," she said.

I must have paused, or had a holoposter expression 'cause next she said, "You were about to ask."

"Could be," I answered.

She smiled and there it began.

She was a student at the uni in town, also an activist, by the content of her conversation. I'd always liked activists not because of any political bent, but because they were called "Anti" same as me. I had never seen an Olmejano student though—at least not one at a uni. I thought the traditions and purification rites wouldn't abide the taint of a US uni considering all the government had done to char the Peruvian forests in which the Olmejano had started.

"So why do they let you go?" I asked.

"No one lets me do anything," she said. I couldn't tell if she was flirting or prickling so I pressed on.

"So you're a convert then? Not born into it? Does that have something to do with the color. You don't wear white." I asked.

"My mother's people are from Eastern Amazonia, yes. But I was born here. Do you know Olmejano markings?"

"Some, but I've never seen any on the neck."

"That's because we're becoming rare."

I waited, but she turned to the dance floor.

"You were about to say?" I ventured.

She looked at me, a slight smile playing at the corners of her mouth.

"I was?"

I had to laugh, though I was becoming a little uncomfortable in my seat. Even if I didn't admit it my body certainly could: I do love a hard ass.

I conceded: "Who is becoming rare?"

"Warriors."

I let that settle in the air, continued.

"Is that what they teach at uni?" I asked.

"There's more than one kind of battle," she responded.

I was talking her into taking me home when the IPD beasts rushed in, weapons drawn. No beeps or warnings. I grabbed her wrist and pulled her up against the smoke bar with me. We ducked under its edge and around the corner. The tender was already through the back door into the kitchen and out to the alley behind. I intended just that route when a shot sizzled over our heads, straight through a row of hookahs and presumably the wall behind. I looked through a gap between the wall and bar to survey the scene. Folks streamed out the exits—windows, doors, some scurried through exposed ductwork in the ceiling just as smooth as years of practice will make you. There looked to be six IPD closing up a circle around a passel of folks who'd been trapped in the middle of the dance floor. Just where I would have been if Xiomarys hadn't caught my attention. One of the IPD wore a captain's blue lapel. My body sweated; I hated the sensation, had never gotten used to leaking at moments like these. Xiomarys lips were at my ear.

"When I tell you, get through that door and into the alley." It sounded like something I might say. It would be followed by a little lie.

"I'll meet you there," she finished.

"There's too many," I said.

"They won't see us," she replied.

"They'll see me and catch you. I know this story. I've told it myself so save the considerate lie because there's too many and you can't be hiding more than a Donnatelli with eighteen shots."

She turned around and looked at me, reappraising.

"There have to be ten people inside that circle plus two of us. We double the IPD." She pulled out a small gun. "And I doubt that I'm the only one armed—maybe someone's even got a Donnatelli."

I didn't doubt that she could make her way out of the grinder and that at least some of the others would make it out. But far as I fathomed blood belonged inside people, us we, folks, or IPD. By then Nestor had taught me that beasts didn't really exist.

"There'll be no need," I said. I looked back through the gap to confirm and closed my eyes. "When I pass out you watch me, still? Make sure nothing else happens."

"What? That—"

Before she could finish I'd pulled myself into the captain's body and lowered his weapon, slipping the safety on as I began.

"Anti," I said pointing at the girl nearest the door, "haven't I seen you before?" The others looked at her from the corner of their eyes, now suspicious. "Aren't you from the Basin?" She looked wary, didn't answer. "Didn't you run from a yes-girl house there?"

From the look on her face she couldn't tell if he was serious or had just made an offer of how to get out in one piece. Her response showed that I'd chosen the right one.

"Yes," she answered. "I've seen you there."

The other IPDs' posture relaxed; they smirked at each other even before I ordered the girl outside. There I had to play it carefully, not stay so long that Xiomarys decided to take action, and also not come close enough to the girl that she'd have a chance to attack me. A woman that will give herself to escape would strike out just as easily for the same reason. I stood next to the window and kept distance between us.

"Go, now." I said.

She didn't hesitate. I counted to fifteen, long enough for her to make it up the block and hail a trans before I reentered the grinder, staggering and cursing, one hand at the captain's belt.

"Fuck!" I stumbled into an officer and turned to him. "Get her! Get her!"

I slipped into her pursuer and left the captain to wonder why he'd done what he'd just done. Outside I waited another count of twenty and yelled. Three more ran out to the street. I phased back in through the window and ran the last man in to a steel girder in the middle of the room and made it back inside myself just in time to slip behind the line of us we slipping out the back door, pulling Xiomarys behind me.

We made it out in a single snaking line that broke apart when we reached the alley. I followed Xiomarys home.

She lived on the top floor of an ancient rowhouse, brick and mortar in the middle of a duocrete city that towered over the squat buildings on her street. When she opened the door and lights glowed on, it looked as if everything were in one room: a small glass and metal desk, disks piled up in stacks and columns around the room, a few paper books and a huge doublethick mattress that took up half of the space. Plants occupied every other open space, seeming to bloom from the walls—tall yellow flowers in one corner, potted trees, and a vine around the window that emitted a light sweet smell that I recognized as her perfume.

The lights dimmed and I heard the zipper of her jacket coming down. When I faced her, the synth fabric of her dress spilled out and stopped to caress the flesh just above her knees. Her eyes sparkled in the dim light.

"You don't even know my name," I said.

"True," she smiled, laid the jacket down on the edge of the bed, "but I have a gun."

I laughed, took off my coat.

She took a step closer to me, looked up the few inches between us.

"What's your name?" she asked.

I told her the truth just to see the look on her face, but she bested me again by stepping closer and laying her mouth against the edge of my jaw, just below the ear.

"Ah, so this is your strength, from such a burden as this."

And something in me slivered and opened.

I had flowed into other women, unable to resist the urge to swell and ebb. I stole their pleasure for my own. But even after I had left them in the morning, I denied the selfishness. I told myself that pleasure, like the moon, drew me to tide and that I only knew how to love in waves.

Xiomarys showed for true the liar I'd been. When she touched me, leaving a trail of tingle across my skin, nothing could have drawn me out of my body. She unbuttoned me, just as cleanly as my shirt and pants that dropped to the floor. Where she kissed, all space between the in and the out, the anchor and the essence evaporated and inside I flowed through myself, only stopping to explode as she took my nipple in her mouth, holding me between her lips, caressing the tip with the warmth of her tongue. Her hands held and caressed all those supple secret places I had forgotten to cherish between journeys and reminded me again why fingers are worthy of worship if attached to the right hands. I kissed her in slow arcs, diving towards the depths of her mouth, the smooth inner flesh of her jaw and back to tease and lick her full lips.

Somehow we reached the bed. There I closed my eyes. Fireflies floated behind my eyelids and remained when I opened them. All sight for the first time melded as I held on, slicked with sweat, and moved against her. Xiomarys kissed down my neck and belly, settled between my thighs. I thought I had been warm. Hot even. Then her tongue lay against me and lapped up in one strong stroke, soft rhythm reaching into me, spreading the knowledge of what bodies are for. Not the running and phasing and fighting that so often make up a life lived out on the forward edge of life, but for sweet lovely this.

To say she fucked me good would only show how little words can do. It can't speak to how I lay there after, looking at the fireflies, still throbbing on what she'd done to me, but aching with every bit of my untouchable flesh for the sensitivity to fade so it could all be done again. All of me drifting on the swell she'd conjured beneath me.

When I came down, and skin didn't feel like fragile silk I turned to her and gave what I got till there wasn't no more to give.

◆◆◆

The next afternoon after a shower and late breakfast, I lounged on Xiomarys's floor going through the disks piled up there. A battered green disk with a black 'X' on its spine sat at the top of one of the stacks. Its label read 'TVA Projects'. Something about it tugged at my memory, a phase a few months before at the archives of the Biogen Bureau.

"You study history?" I asked
"Among other things, yes," she answered.
"TVA?" I asked.
"Tennessee—"
It clicked.
"Valley Authority" I finished.
"You know it?" she asked, looking at me playfully.
"Could be."
She rested her chin in her hand and grinned at me.
"Mind if I look?" I asked.
She walked over to me, golden skin glowing, long legs under a short shirt and placed her hand over mine, tugging gently.
"Let me show you," she said
"Show me?"
"For now, the reader."
I sat at her desk and waited while she loaded the disk and tilted the top tier of the glass toward me.
This is the story that Mama Myrtha had told me:
Years ago, the mouth of the Tennessee River could no longer contain itself and exploded forth, filling the valley below with its collected knowledge of contaminants, unique species, and impressive contortions of drift wood. The valley lay there and tried to take it in. This was a brave, but ultimately stupid attempt. As most relationships, the Tennessee consumed it and moved on to the next. Our home had been the jewel of the valley; the waters teemed with creatures not found anywhere else in the world; even the rocks held treasure. During the floods everything got mixed in together—more mixed than the gene adaptations even. We were cut off and those outside, surrendered to jealousy and fear. They built a fence to try and contain everything that lived on land and in the water. They stopped speaking of that place and waited for it to fade into legend, all the time still searching for the magic that terrified them.

It was a pretty story that I never quite believed; it turns out that parts of it were true.

The fence around the Basin had been ordered into existence shortly after the last great flood in the Tennessee River Basin swept over the TVA dams, surpassed the locks and ruined what had once been Chattanooga and many of the surrounding counties of Eastern Tennessee. All this so that the greater Mississippi Basin wouldn't be jeopardized—or so was the official story. Dozens of mountains had been leveled off in mining during the previous fifty years. So a series of floods overwhelmed the area. Species of freshwater mussels and fish only found there mutated or became extinct. All the while abandoned mines flooded and drained many times over further destabilizing the underlying bedrock. This created my home, the Basin, unique in its inhabitants and all they had lived through. Though biogen adaptations had become common, the IPD still worried that our tricks might be handier than theirs. I didn't need the disk to tell me that. It described the quarantine as only affecting water species who might be carrying contagion after long exposure to raw sewage, industrial contaminants, and mine runoff that had seeped into the Basin after the floods. The content on the disks was decades old. Xiomarys had apparently found them buried at a library sale. The librarians couldn't tell her anymore than was on the disk. The subject matter was 'low demand' they said and would probably not be replaced or preserved in the upcoming budget cuts. That was as much as they knew or cared about those last remnants of the TVA collection. The Basin was no more real to them than the antiquarian battles of Greece.

I knew how real it was. And keeping us we well fed and warm in a cage wouldn't ever equal freedom.

I told Xiomarys I wasn't feeling well, laid down, and closed my eyes. I went not to sleep but to work. I had enough information to take the next step: TVA. Three letters that I could use to find where the Basin and all us we had been filed away and forgotten.

I phased one person to another and found the right man in just three hours.

♦♦♦

Tressidor Donovan made lists all the time, constructing his short-term purpose. As if he could validate his life if there was enough paperwork to document it. With a few exceptions, he led a happy life. Directly after an unremarkable college career he had found the perfect job: third staff coordinator for internal security, barriers division. He didn't seem particularly aware that he was in charge of fences that kept thousands of people on a range of buttes that according to Xiomarys's disks had once been mountains. Caught up in the flow of figures and forms from one department to another, the actual impact of Tressidor's work escaped him. It didn't register in his conscious or unconscious mind, an irrelevant detail against the backdrop of his lists. When I first settled in I didn't know how I could reach into all that data and pull out the information that might convince him to disrupt his routine.

I found the answer more easily than I ever could have imagined. I just looked in the back and found the things he wanted to do before he died:

Make love to a hairy man
See the Great Barrier Reef
Stand up to Mr. Newcastle
Climb Mt. Shasta

Mr. Newcastle, Tressidor's supervisor and a short pig of a man walked into the office just as we finished booking the shuttle ticket from Reno to Mt. Shasta.

"Tress," (Tressidor swore under his breath) "I was just going over your report and it looks as if you've failed to check the math on your last HO3-R. If you'll look here . . ."

Newcastle walked around the desk and sat on the edge a few inches from Tressidor's shoulder, pushing back the picture of Tressidor's wife with his ass. The HO3-R wasn't an official form. Mr. Newcastle had created it as a supplement to the HO3-Q that Tressidor had designed to replace three other forms with redundant information. Upon review, the steering committee and approval board confirmed Tressidor's form and circulated it to other departments. Not to be outdone by an subordinate Mr. Newcastle had required that his own creation, the HO3-R, unreviewed and unapproved, be included in all sub-intradepartmental communications. The approval board didn't know about the form, but Newcastle threw a fit if it wasn't included in every quarterly report.

With Mr. Newcastle's significant body odor spreading throughout the small cubicle space, Tressidor decided to cross Mr. Newcastle off his list right then and there. I watched, wondering what form his rebellion would take. He didn't turn to the Newcastle and start cursing him; point out the obvious flaws in the Ho3-R including logical errors wherein barriers could be deauthorized for a myriad of nonsensical reasons including retroactive self-generated math errors and lack of paper weight approval; or even rescue his wife's framed photo from the proximity of Newcastle's ass. Tressidor quietly nodded at the right moments and let Newcastle walk away, a smug look of incompetence smeared across his face. Tressidor went back to work on the form, filling it out incorrectly per cover sheet instructions and then turned back to the pile of acquisitions and mandates disks that he'd been updating before his boss's interruption. I guessed that he'd delayed his stand until I turned my attention to the forms he filled in with the speed and precision of a microprocessor.

At the bottom of the screen it read: "Destruction of Barrier Fence 214-224, TVA-Q: Authorized." He appended Newcastle's

HO3-R to the transmission and pressed 'Confirm', sending it to the unit head with the rest of the quarter's reports.

Inside him, a small window opened and a list was sucked outside, revealing a pristine open space underneath.

❖❖❖

The next day I phased into a woman from IPD's Basin Surveillance department to look through the cameras that had spied on me all those years. I sat down at her station and punched in the coordinates for the TVA-Q perimeter surveillance system. When the images came on screen I learned something that I hadn't encountered in 19 years of phasing: I could make someone cry for my emotion. Two errant tears ran down the IPD woman's face. A sob hitched in her throat as more tears began to flow, blurring my vision. The coworker beside her asked if she was all right. She wiped her eyes and said she didn't know why she was crying. I knew why. I had already seen the image.

The fence posts around the perimeter were gone. Government crews had already loaded the last of the fencing in heavy gray trucks and driven them back to storage. The omnipresent holo of Burke surveyed the scene: Us we muddled about, only 15 meters further out than they once had. And most had already turned back toward the Basin and home. There was no other discernable change.

I came back to myself as quickly as I could. My body still rested in Xiomarys's bed. The tears fell before I could catch them, pooling into my ears. I didn't have the strength to move or even turn to the wall. I didn't see Xiomarys sitting at the desk reading, but when she rose and came to me, relief flooded through me.

When she touched me I let every secret drop from my lips. Of course she didn't believe I could do what I did until I entered her. After, she looked at me in a way I couldn't place. I'd exposed myself now; I didn't see the use in stopping.

"And that flooding holo staring down from the sky at my failure. All that time it was like we were being watched—not just by the IPD, or each other, but by this man none of us had ever met or would ever meet. Like the feds were watching us in our beds, all behind this guise of a great man who never meant us anything but harm. Do you know they beam his speeches in to the Basin? Can't dredge up the tech to keep the necessities in, but we can all be boomed out of bed by speeches that pretend we don't exist. He never talked about us or defended our right to the pursuit of happiness and genetic survival like all those rich folks who are always in his commercials. And those folks believe everything he says. Every lie he tells. Thinking that he's really running anything."

"It's not that they believe him," Xiomarys responded. "They believe in him, in the President and they still do. They have to—if they don't then what have they been believing in? What other lies have they believed? They don't even believe in the Basin, because they don't want to.

"I don't even know who 'they' is anymore," I said.

I knew that though I may be able to pull parts of me from one body to the next, in my own skin-tall, brown, and strong— I'm still invisible. And not just me, but all us we in the Basin, the Olmejano in the charred forests, and all the poor or restricted people in the spaces between. All us are hidden from each other.

I can pull down fences with the help of individual hands, but it won't bring us closer together. Fences still stay up in people's minds.

I had to find another way.

◆◆◆

Wesley Burke was elected President because his first cousin twice removed was made to play at slave for a week. Even after six decades, the image of Kristen Burke, a senator's child and socialite, chained and dirty, wiping away at invisible cobwebs and babbling her gratitude for a bit of food hadn't faded into the annals of history. It didn't matter that the government had hunted down and executed nearly every member of the radical group that had kidnapped her and the other senators' children. Every year they dragged the static electronic file out and played it like prayer, after every riot and every UN meeting about the US's human rights record. When a Burke finally ran for public office, rich folks couldn't wait to vote him into office, and so they kept doing it until he ended up President less than a decade after starting his political career.

I was able to enter him because a brave doctor gave my ancestors genetic reparations for their ancestor's slavery—twice removed. Dead don't fear no death 'cause nothing ever dies; it's just transformed into intention, tradition, the way we treat one another.

One could say the remnants of righteous indignation fueled both of our trajectories.

Out in the oblong amphitheater of what had been the eastern ridge of the Laguna Mountains, before the wildfires of the 2070s, President Burke stood before a throng of supporters gathered in a multitude of standing deadwood, California tinder, covering the hills around them.

"These stately trees will be the sentinels of rebirth. Andor Technologies will bring the future through these hills and to the good people of California and the Mexicali States, cheaper, faster and bigger than ever before."

Up on stage, Burke wore a sleek gray suit with no tie, his shoes worth more than most family's yearly salary, looking every bit the fearless, distant leader, wavy graying hair lifted by the slight breeze. He wore his jacket unbuttoned so that the strap of his trademark holster could be seen when he gestured toward a scraggly line of genetically-engineered saplings.

In second sight, he didn't resemble the man at the podium or in the holoposters at all. He only had a glow. It faded away at the edges, more an impression than a presence, but at his center a spark flickered arhythmically, like a light in a fog. I waited until his speech was over to phase into him. After the last bit of pomp and shite dropped from his lips, I pulled myself into the space between flickers. Luckily, he was already stepping down from the stage so the Secret Service agents around him took the change as no more than a stumble. The closest one caught him before he hit the ground. Inside, I had to slip around him and down into an empty space that gaped in its vastness. If it were a different man I would have worried for him and wanted to find the memories behind all that empty, to know what he was hiding from himself, covering with willful disregard, but in Burke I didn't have to wonder long or peer under the empty.

You might think that anger is hot, or maybe hatred, but in every body I've been inside guilt throws off heat like an engine; it also tends to run things. Finding such an abundance of it in Burke made me hope that I could reach him.

I stayed quiet and watched, didn't go searching through his memories and delving into his intentions. I waited for him to acknowledge me so I could tell him what I've told you.

He tried to ignore me, but soon he couldn't. Later that afternoon we sat at his desk while his press secretary and the Vice President carefully laid out his stance on every issue on the current environmental agenda. When the President didn't respond, they didn't seem to notice. Their conversation never faltered as they made notes in thin black agendas and exchanged laughs at everyone else's expense.

Inside the President, I whispered that the time had come for truth. I told him the only words worthy of that microphone and podium he seemed so fond of were ones that started with the facts. He spoke as little to me as he did to them. With every sentence, the temperature seemed to drop until my words puffed out in clouds of steam that floated off into the distance.

Suddenly the President stood up, knocking his chair backwards, antique casters spinning in the air.

"Mr. President?" The press secretary said.

"Wes," the VP said, a look of thinly masked disdain surfacing, "Wes, you're scaring Bradley. Why don't you take your seat?"

Burke looked down at the VP, his hands spastically clenching to fists and relaxing.

"Goddammit—" was all Burke could get out. I walked him around the desk and sat in him on the corner of it.

The press secretary excused himself and left the VP to speak with Burke. The VP stood and stepped toward the President. He sighed and took a cigar out of the humidifier on the president's desk.

"Look Wes, I don't know what's going on with you, but you have to pull it together." The VP cut the end of the cigar off and left it on the carpet where it settled after bouncing off of Burke's shoe. He leaned closer.

"People are depending on you to do your goddamn job, Wes. You do remember what that is, don't you?" He looked into Burke's eyes, expecting an answer and by the tone in his voice, a rote one. I searched Burke's mind for the right response. Inside, a curse seeped from the corner of his mind that I'd placed him in. And as the answer came to me, the chill of resentment tempered Burke's heat. A vibration passed.

"I do the talking," I said with the President's voice, trying to keep incredulity out of it.

"Yes, that's right you do the talking. There's a team of people to do the planning. And I'll do the maneuvering, Wes. It's worked for 7 years and once the amendment goes through a lot more years. So no outbursts in front of reporters, dignitaries, or the staff, not even some secretary with a nice ass. Just keep your wife in line and stop choosing your own words. If you lose credibility, there's nothing left for you to do in this organization." The VP was inhaling deeply now, enjoying the sound of his voice as he admonished the head of state, dropping ashes on his carpet. "I don't want that to happen. I'm on your side, Wes, so work with me, okay?"

This seemed to give the President some comfort. He relaxed a bit, cursed less from his corner. Warmth started to seep back inside.

The VP strolled out the door, the smell of his smoke still thick in the room. I could still smell it as I lay in the President that night, tired but unwilling to leave him until I could make him understand what must be done.

I have never liked inhabiting sleeping people. Their dreams can overwhelm, like being caught in a hallucination. Wesley Burke's dreams staggered even more than this: he was a lucid dreamer. He controlled every aspect of this internal world—as if here he compensated for all the power he should have had on the outside. He changed environments and players at whim, stopped time and rewound it, playing out different endings until the next scenario zoomed into focus. Watching, I stood in the corner struggling to take in all the things around me. I had hoped that I could reach him here, that he might still consider choosing to tell his own secrets, or rather the country's. The guilt inside him made me believe that he knew that forced ignorance worked to no one's benefit. I waited for a quiet moment between battles, orgies, and murder mysteries to say my piece.

A scene of a lake shimmered into focus and it looked like the time had finally come. Burke kneeled at the water's edge, next to a large weeping willow, gazing down into the water. I thought he might flee if I faced him so I approached from behind. I stepped heavy so that he would hear me coming but as close as I came, his attention stayed on the water. I followed his gaze. A city was visible just under the surface. It was laid out as cleanly as the capital, the same buildings and streets shrunk down and sunken. I'd seen such visions before: the desert that had been home, a mudslide on a sunny day, endless winters and ceaseless summers. Inside folks minds I'd seen hurricanes wipe land barren and recognized the images repeated in holocasts and updates. It didn't surprise me to see this in Burke. Fears of common disasters, inhabited a lot of folks—especially those who had helped me along the way. As I closed the distance between us, I hoped a bit more that he would do the talking and I could just lay back inside him while he, for once, spoke the truth.

His shoulders gently shook as he leaned closer to the edge, one hand reaching out to touch the water. I was right behind him now and could see clearly. What I had mistaken for a lake was something else, still clear and round but covered by a translucent barrier that rippled and shifted with the wind. Bubbles rose to the underside as breath collected in pockets. I squinted trying to decipher. When I understood I took an unconscious step back.

There were people in the water, small as tadpoles. They swam away from the great city and toward the surface, moving straight to Burke or rather a small space in front of him, a hole where fresh air flowed. Shaking, he leaned forward and covered the hole, watching as their limp bodies floated back down to the buildings, the streets and lawns, filling the city.

Even up close, I could not tell if he laughed or cried. But he did not stop—could not stop.

After that, I did not speak to the President, did not move his hand or try to ply him with soft words. There was nothing in him to appeal to. He would not change; his good was lost and, with it, my modicum of faith in him. But the people I had been inside craved change. And I was ready to give it to them. Words may not have been able to move Burke, but others would listen. If he wouldn't speak the truth then I could use his voice and speak it myself.

♦♦♦

Much as I can see when I'm inside a person, I only know what's already articulated, built up strong in them. Half-done things are just as shapeless inside as out. Maybe I should have realized what Burke would do from that first day when he chose to fall rather than to walk with me. He put the muzzle of his gun to his head, aiming at me. He pulled the trigger, staying forever in control of himself.

But control is nothing like you think it is. Only so much can be anticipated. I couldn't know Burke's choice just as I couldn't know that a beam splitter could make me more, in number and magnitude, than I've ever been. I hadn't ever encountered either before.

When I bolted into the splitter's path I felt myself coming apart, getting turned inside, all of it too quick to feel fear, only the warmth of being bared. Each person that I entered was like a light turned on in an expansive night, all of it building into a dawn as they entered my life, my story, this moment we now share.

Sometimes it's the damndest thing, what you can't fathom that saves you.

◆◆◆

During yesterday's State of the Union address in front of USTV, WorldSpan, the BBC and every news organization in the country, the President committed suicide. Fifteen minutes later you could have turned on a vid in Tonga, Tonga and watched the gray matter explode from his temple, seen the shiny silver 9mm catch the bright broadcast lights and blind the unblinking eye for a moment.

But you would not have seen everything that transpired, not countless people who fell silent as a life not their own flashed before their eyes.

There was footage of the aftermath. In it, news crews, pedestrians, government workers, street people, and more queued up from all over the capitol, moving toward a rundown street on the Southeast quadrant. The people made no noise as they walked through the streets. For a long time, no one acknowledged each other or even spoke. Many congregated on a tiny lawn in front of a nondescript row house. The rest stared up at a window on the top floor, rapt, as if waiting.

◆◆◆

Dead rose, slowly, on to her elbow. Soft, cool sheets surrounded her; a slight breeze blew in from the window ruffling the plants near the bed. She knew all this though her eyes remained shut. She savored the sensations, but none more than the woman who lay next to her, breath on her neck, hand in hers. Xiomarys reached out to touch her cheek. And for a moment, one she would never divulge, she thought of Nina and an afternoon they'd spent learning how a thousand pieces can be whole and still be brought back together—until now the only real magic Dead had ever known. A sound had roused Dead from the deep meditation that had followed her last phase. For hours she lay here collecting herself, as each of the people gathered outside brought an errant bit back to its center. But now something wafted in from the street enticing her from her reverie: the sound of voices rising, perhaps as one.

About the Authors

J. D. EveryHope, originally from Bellingham WA, now studies at Sarah Lawrence College in New York. She spends her time researching comparative mythology, medieval history, and other subjects mostly irrelevant to twenty-first century life. Whenever she's not doodling or being attacked by manic cats, she writes and drinks far too much coffee. She hopes to pursue a career as a professional writer, and failing that, intends to spend her days drawing on the walls of a cardboard box in Central Park.

❖❖❖

Tenea D. Johnson is a writer and musician. Her work has appeared in African Voices, Arise, Humanities in the South, Infinite Matrix, Necrologue and Whispers in the Night, among others. Some years ago she stopped separating music from fiction, ended up with fusions and trotted them out at the Knitting Factory, Dixon Place, and the Public Theater. She is also the mother of a bouncing baby label, counterpoise records. You can reach her at tdj@teneadjohnson.com.

❖❖❖

Dr. Philip Edward Kaldon teaches Physics at Western Michigan University in Kalamazoo by day, while aspiring to write The Great Science Fiction Romantic Epic in the wee hours of the night. In 2008, his SF story "A Man in the Moon" appeared in the Writers of the Future Vol. XXIV and he has stories coming out in Analog and Andromeda Spaceways Inflight Magazine. Dr. Phil attended the 2004 Clarion workshop with Blind Eye Books editor Nikki Kimberling and also the August 2008 Writers of the Future workshop and event with Jemma EveryHope, who helped edit this story. He turns fifty this year and met his wife Debbie in the Science and Engineering Library at Northwestern University – they've been married for just about a quarter century, which does not impress their three cats.

❖❖❖

About the Authors

Erin MacKay was born in Mobile, Alabama and raised all over the southeastern United States. She lives in Atlanta with her husband and two dogs. Her interests include history, linguistics, gourmet beer, football, and anime, not necessarily in that order.

❖❖❖

Trent Roman is a writer from Montréal with an interest in all types of fiction strange and unusual in addition to academic interests in archaeology, anthropology, history and a number of other fields. He is fascinated by what makes people tick at both the intimately personal level and the sweeping societal level, and enjoys every opportunity to pursue such questions through the means of fiction. Other publications where Roman's stories have or will appear are listed at his cruddy website, www.geocities.com/trent_roman/

❖❖❖

Jesse Sandoval was born and raised in New Mexico. He plays guitar better than he writes.